NO OTHER WAY

WILLOW ROSE

Cover design by Juan Villar Padron,
https://www.juanjpadron.com

Special thanks to my editor Janell Parque
http://janellparque.blogspot.com/

**To be the first to hear about new releases and
bargains from Willow Rose, sign up below to be
on the VIP List.** (I promise not to share your email with
anyone else, and I won't clutter your inbox.)

- GO HERE TO SIGN UP TO BE ON THE VIP LIST :
http://readerlinks.com/l/415254

Tired of too many emails? Text the word: "willowrose" to 31996 to sign up to Willow's VIP text List to
get a text alert with news about New Releases, Giveaways,
Bargains and Free books from Willow.

Books by the Author

MYSTERY/THRILLER/HORROR NOVELS

- IN ONE FELL SWOOP
- UMBRELLA MAN
- BLACKBIRD FLY
- TO HELL IN A HANDBASKET
- EDWINA

HARRY HUNTER MYSTERY SERIES

- ALL THE GOOD GIRLS
- RUN GIRL RUN

MARY MILLS MYSTERY SERIES

- WHAT HURTS THE MOST
- YOU CAN RUN
- YOU CAN'T HIDE
- CAREFUL LITTLE EYES

EVA RAE THOMAS MYSTERY SERIES

- DON'T LIE TO ME
- WHAT YOU DID
- NEVER EVER
- SAY YOU LOVE ME
- LET ME GO

EMMA FROST SERIES

- Itsy Bitsy Spider
- Miss Dolly had a Dolly
- Run, Run as Fast as You Can
- Cross Your Heart and Hope to Die
- Peek-a-Boo I See You
- Tweedledum and Tweedledee
- Easy as One, Two, Three
- There's No Place like Home
- Slenderman
- Where the Wild Roses Grow
- Waltzing Mathilda
- Drip Drop Dead

JACK RYDER SERIES

- Hit the Road Jack
- Slip out the Back Jack
- The House that Jack Built
- Black Jack
- Girl Next Door
- Her Final Word
- Don't Tell

REBEKKA FRANCK SERIES

- One, Two...He is Coming for You
- Three, Four...Better Lock Your Door
- Five, Six...Grab your Crucifix
- Seven, Eight...Gonna Stay up Late
- Nine, Ten...Never Sleep Again
- Eleven, Twelve...Dig and Delve
- Thirteen, Fourteen...Little Boy Unseen
- Better Not Cry
- Ten Little Girls

- IT ENDS HERE

HORROR SHORT-STORIES

- MOMMY DEAREST
- THE BIRD
- BETTER WATCH OUT
- EENIE, MEENIE
- ROCK-A-BYE BABY
- NIBBLE, NIBBLE, CRUNCH
- HUMPTY DUMPTY
- CHAIN LETTER

PARANORMAL SUSPENSE/ROMANCE NOVELS

- IN COLD BLOOD
- THE SURGE
- GIRL DIVIDED

THE VAMPIRES OF SHADOW HILLS SERIES

- FLESH AND BLOOD
- BLOOD AND FIRE
- FIRE AND BEAUTY
- BEAUTY AND BEASTS
- BEASTS AND MAGIC
- MAGIC AND WITCHCRAFT
- WITCHCRAFT AND WAR
- WAR AND ORDER
- ORDER AND CHAOS

- CHAOS AND COURAGE

THE AFTERLIFE SERIES

- BEYOND
- SERENITY
- ENDURANCE
- COURAGEOUS

THE WOLFBOY CHRONICLES

- A GYPSY SONG
- I AM WOLF

DAUGHTERS OF THE JAGUAR

- SAVAGE
- BROKEN

STATEMENT OF KRISTIN HOLMES

INCIDENT # 2010-141345

CARSON: Today's date is April 15[th,] 2010; the current time is 1209 hours. I am Detective Gary Carson, along with Sergeant Steve Bailey. We're here at Monroe County Sheriff's Office at 5525 College Road, Key West. We're talking to Kristin regarding the disappearance of Kate Taylor, who was last seen on April 13[th,] 2010, at Sloppy Joe's Bar at three a.m. All right, uh, Kristin, would you mind repeating your name and spelling it for me, please?

KRISTIN: Oh, okay. My name is, uh, Kristin Holmes. That is K-R-I-S-T-I-N H-O-L-M-E-S.

CARSON: All right. And what do you do, Kristin?

KRISTIN: I am a therapist. Pediatric therapist.

CARSON: All right. Now, Kristin. Tell us why you are here.

KRISTIN: Well, I was, uh, me and my two friends were…

CARSON: (Fiddles with pages, then moves microphone) That is Joan Smith and Kate Taylor, right?

KRISTIN: Right.

CARSON: Go on. Please, speak into the microphone.

KRISTIN: Well, we wanted to go on this trip, this road trip, to Key West and Key Largo. It was Kate's thirty-fifth birthday, and we wanted to treat her to something, uh, special, and so we thought we'd come down here to party and then later swim with dolphins. All Kate wanted was to try that, so we thought this was the time.

CARSON: Without your husbands? You live in Miami, right?

KRISTIN: Well, I'm not married, but the other two are, and yes. We all live in Miami. Kate needed to get away on her own for a little.

CARSON: And why is that?

KRISTIN: Well, she… I don't know, she was… she and Andrew have been fighting a lot lately; I don't know the details, but she told me she really needed to get away.

CARSON: Do you think she was scared of him?

KRISTIN: (long pause) No. I think she was just bummed out about the marriage. She never told us much about it, just that she needed to blow off some steam or something like that.

CARSON: Was that the term she used? Blow off some steam?

KRISTIN: (sighs deeply) I don't…I don't remember exactly how she put it, but yes, that was the idea. To get away.

CARSON: Okay. And then what happened?

KRISTIN: Well, we drove the long way down here and spent the first night at some hotel downtown, then went to the sunset festival and later Sloppy Joe's.

CARSON: Did Kate meet anyone there? Talk to anyone?

KRISTIN: (sniffles) She talked to a bunch of people. It's how she is, you know? She likes to talk to people.

CARSON: Was there anyone in particular that she spoke with?

KRISTIN: (long pause) Well, there was this guy, uh, but I don't think that…

CARSON: And this guy, can you give us a description? Did he give her his name?

KRISTIN: Matt, his name was Matt. That was all she told us. He was tall, had brown hair and blue eyes. A little young, in my opinion, but Kate liked him.

CARSON: And what did Matt and Kate do?

KRISTIN: They danced and maybe they, uh, kissed a little.

CARSON: Uh-huh, and what else?

KRISTIN: What do you mean?

CARSON: Did she sleep with him?

KRISTIN: (pauses) Well, no, I don't think so. We all had a little too much to drink, so I don't really know. She was all over him, though, and kept saying she was crazy about him. She could have gone off at some point and… you know, without us knowing it.

CARSON: Is Kate the type who would do that?

KRISTIN: Yes.

CARSON: But she didn't go home with him?

KRISTIN: No, she wouldn't do that. She was supposed to come back to the hotel with us. We were going to leave early in the morning to go to Key Largo and swim with the dolphins.

CARSON: But you never made it that far? You never made it to Key Largo, and you didn't go swimming with dolphins?

KRISTIN: (Sniffles) No. She wasn't in her bed the next morning. We think she never came back to the hotel. She stayed longer at Sloppy's than Joan and me.

CARSON: And that was two days ago, right?

KRISTIN: Right. At first, we thought she might have gone somewhere, maybe gone home with this Matt guy, and we waited for her to come back, calling her phone, but she didn't pick up. When she didn't come back last night, we went to the police, to you, and said we couldn't find her. We filed a missing person's report, and the officers on duty said they'd look for her. They also said she was probably out partying still and that she'd show up eventually, that they got a lot of disappearance cases like this, especially around spring break. Usually, they'd show up on their own. We went looking for her everywhere around town. Then, you called us this morning and told us to come in at noon.

CARSON: And you have no idea where she could have gone? She hasn't hinted anything or maybe told you something like she wanted to run away or anything like that?

KRISTIN: I don't know. Maybe.

CARSON: What does that mean?

KRISTIN: She did tell me once in the car on the way here that she wished she could just disappear. But people say stuff like that, right?

CARSON: Some people might, but very few actually do it. Now, did she leave a note, a text, or anything?

KRISTIN: No. We called Andrew, and he hadn't heard from her either. He's on his way down here now.

CARSON: Okay, Kristin. Is there anything you'd like to add to your statement?

KRISTIN: I don't think so. I'm just…I'm really worried about her, you know?

CARSON: Okay. All right, Kristin, uh, I'm going to go ahead and conclude this interview for now. It's 1250 hours.

STATEMENT OF JOAN SMITH

INCIDENT # 2010-141345

CARSON: Today's date is April 15th, 2010; the current time is 1304 hours. I am Detective Gary Carson, along with Sergeant Steve Bailey at Monroe County Sheriff's Office at 5525 College Road, Key West. We're talking to Joan Smith regarding the disappearance of Kate Taylor, who was last seen on April 13th, 2010. Joan, do you mind repeating your name and spelling it for me, please?

JOAN: Joan Smith, J-O-A-N S-M-I-T-H.

CARSON: And what do you do, Joan? What's your profession?

JOAN: Me? I don't do anything (laughs nervously). I am what you'd call a professional housewife. My husband is a lawyer in Miami. I take care of the kiddos, is what I do. But between you and me, I'd much rather be working.

CARSON: And what can you tell me about the reason that you're here today?

JOAN: Well, you asked me to come in, didn't you? I was hoping it was because you would help me look for Kate.

CARSON: That's what we're trying to do.

JOAN: So…? Have you looked for her?

CARSON: We have patrols out searching for her.

JOAN: So, why are we here?

CARSON: Tell me about why you've come to the Keys.

JOAN: Kate wanted to do something special for her birthday; it's her thirty-fifth, so she's beginning to feel a little old, you know? She wanted to have fun, go out for a night with the girls, then drive up to Key Largo and swim with dolphins.

CARSON: But she didn't want to go with her husband, and I believe she has a child too?

JOAN: Yes, and no. She needed some time off, some time to herself. Us girls need that every now and then too, you know? Just like the boys need to hang out and belch at the TV or look at women in a bar.

CARSON: Were you coming here to look at men?

JOAN: Heck, yeah. Kate needed to see something other than that dull husband of hers. She needed to feel wanted again.

CARSON: And her husband didn't make her feel wanted?

JOAN: Listen, Andrew is as sweet as the day is long, but he is just as dull too. She was tired of him and wanted to blow off some steam. Who can blame her?

CARSON: Blow off some steam? Was that the term she used?

JOAN: I guess. Maybe not in those words, but that was the gist of it, yes. She wanted to get away.

CARSON: Get away from what exactly?

JOAN: I think she was just bummed out about the marriage. She never told me much about it, but I know when a girlfriend is in a bad marriage.

CARSON: So, was it a bad marriage?

JOAN: No more than most marriages, I guess. No more than mine. We all have our issues, don't we?

CARSON: But she wanted out of her marriage, is that it?

JOAN: Yes, she said so several times. She wanted to get away.

CARSON: Could her husband have hurt her?

JOAN: Andrew? No, please. He is many things, but violent is not one of them.

CARSON: Is he the jealous type?

JOAN: What do you mean?

CARSON: Would he get angry if she was unfaithful?

JOAN: She would never do that. Not Kate.

CARSON: So, she didn't cheat on him?

JOAN: No.

CARSON: That isn't her character?

JOAN: She wouldn't.

CARSON: She didn't meet anyone while you were down here?

JOAN: No.

CARSON: She didn't talk to anyone while you were partying?

JOAN: She talked to a lot of people. Kate loved to talk to people.

CARSON: But no one in particular? There wasn't one person she spoke to or danced with?

JOAN: No. I don't think so. I would have noticed if she spoke to someone in particular.

CARSON: (papers rustling) Because your other friend mentioned a man, someone named Matt? Does that name ring a bell?

JOAN: (pauses, then chuckles nervously) Ah, Matt, that guy, yes. I forgot about him.

CARSON: Can you describe him?

JOAN: I don't know, uhm, he was bald, I think, or maybe that was some other guy.

CARSON: So, you don't remember what he looked like?

JOAN: We had a lot to drink. I'm sorry; I don't. I don't think Kate liked him very much, and she got rid of him quickly.

CARSON: (clears throat) Did she ever talk about leaving her husband?

JOAN: Yes. I think she was tired of him. She did say in the car on the way here that she wished she could just disappear.

CARSON: So, you think that's what happened? She just left?

JOAN: (long pause) How the heck am I supposed to know? All I know is that she wasn't in her bed the next morning like she was supposed to be. We shared a room and thought she'd come home on her own. She didn't want to go back with us, so we left her there at the bar. At first, we thought she might have gone somewhere, and we waited for her to come back, calling her phone, but she didn't answer. After we had waited for a very long time and she didn't come back, we went to the police and said we couldn't find her. We filed a missing person's report, and the officers on duty said they'd look for her. They also said she was probably out partying still and that she'd show up eventually. Then, you called us this morning and told us to come in at noon.

CARSON: Okay, Joan. I think we're about done here. Is there anything you'd like to add to your statement?

JOAN: I don't think so.

CARSON: Okay. All right. I'm going to go ahead and conclude this interview for now. It's 1402 hours.

TEN YEARS LATER

Chapter 1

MY DAD WAVED from the front pew, and we rushed up next to him. Josie plopped down in the seat next to me with an annoyed sigh, staring at her phone from underneath the pulled-up hoodie.

"What took you so long? It's about to start," my dad said.

"I'll have to tell you later."

I glared at Josie, then shook my head. She had an outfit breakdown this morning. That was why we were late for church. Those weren't unusual these days, but today had been worse than the other times. She had cried and said she looked stupid in everything and that she felt like a hobo because she was wearing sweatpants. I told her not to wear sweatpants, that it was silly anyway because it was eighty degrees outside.

"But I want to wear them," she had answered.

"Then wear them. I think you look great."

"Are you kidding me? I look like a homeless person, or some druggie," she had then said.

I had stared at her in confusion, not knowing what to

say next. It didn't matter what I tried to say anyway. It would be wrong, no matter what. So, I had shut up, with the result that she had growled at me and told me I didn't care about her. In the end, I had just told her to get a move on, probably yelling it a little too loudly. And here we were, almost missing the beginning of the service.

Yes, it was true what they said. Age fourteen is a nightmare year for a girl. I had never had a boy, so I couldn't say what that was like, but this girl was enough teenager for me for the time being.

It'll pass. She'll grow older and then it'll get better.

The worship music began, and we rose to our feet. Josie stayed sitting, and my dad noticed, then pushed my arm and nodded toward her.

I leaned down so she could hear me. "Josie, stand up, please."

"Why?" she whined. "I don't like this music."

"We're at church, and we stand up and worship just as we stand in respect for God's word. Come."

"I can't. My legs hurt."

"Your legs hurt?"

"From volleyball, remember? Besides, I can worship just fine while sitting down. God doesn't care."

I took a deep breath, trying to remain calm. She had been testing my patience for the past few weeks, and to be honest, I was getting a little tired of it.

"Josie, I need you to get up right now and put that phone away. Now."

"But…"

"Josie!"

"I just don't understand why I can't just sit down and…"

I gave her a look, *that* look, the one letting her know she had reached the end of the rope. If she continued, she knew that she'd end up getting grounded and her phone privileges taken away.

Reluctantly, she put the phone in the pocket of her hoodie, then rose to her feet. I took in another deep breath, feeling everything but victorious, then closed my eyes.

God, I need all the strength you can give me today. Please. And tomorrow too and the rest of the week while you're at it. I have no idea how to deal with this all by myself.

Josie's mother, my wife Camille, had overdosed three years ago and was left with a brain injury that she was still trying to recover from. She had started rehabilitation, and I had hired a fulltime nurse for her, even though both were way above my budget. She had regained some of her speech and mobility but was still bound to a wheelchair. For three years she was bedridden and in a vegetative state until two months earlier when she suddenly woke up, and we started to communicate with her. She still only said a few words, but her vocabulary was slowly growing, and she was beginning to understand more of what we told her.

But we still didn't know exactly what happened to her. She had recently managed to communicate to me that someone had tried to kill her, but we hadn't come any closer as to who or why.

I, for one, was determined to do everything in my power to find out and bring them to justice.

My favorite worship song was next, and I sang along while tears ran down my cheeks. I was so grateful to God for bringing my wife back and for getting my daughter a new heart when she needed it. But there was still so much I didn't understand, and I felt my faith diminishing as the days passed.

When God, when? When will we get the answers we need? When will these people be brought to justice?

The worst part was that I had also recently discovered

that my wife wasn't who I thought she was. I had stopped a group of human traffickers, taking down a group of my colleagues, smuggling refugees through Miami Harbor from South America and the Caribbean inside appliances. But before he had killed himself, one of the guys I believed was in charge had told me Camille played a role in this. Or that she at least knew it was happening and who was behind it. I wondered now if that was why they had tried to kill her.

The only person I shared these things with was my neighbor, Jean. She was a nurse and had helped us out from the beginning once Camille got sick. She used to be best friends with Camille, but now she was so much more than that. She was family, and to me, she was even more than that. I had realized I was falling for her, and that maybe I had been in love with her for a long time. But as Camille woke up, I had to distance myself from her, so I wouldn't hurt her. Still, she was the only one I trusted enough to share my thoughts with, even though I tried not to.

When did life get so complicated?

I wiped the tears off my cheeks and looked briefly at my dad, who worshipped with his hands in the air, eyes closed, and sang his dear heart out. My dad was my rock, and without him, I wouldn't have been able to go through all this. He helped me when in need, and as a former pastor, he was always ready with an uplifting and faith-building word for me when I struggled, which was a lot these days.

The music stopped, and the pastor took the stage.

"Give it up for our worship team," he said. "Aren't they amazing?"

People clapped. Josie had sat back down and was on her phone once again. I decided not to say anything. The last thing I wanted was for her to hate going to church as she got older. I had to pick my battles with her at this age; my dad had taught me that. It was easier said than done, but I was trying to live by it.

"Please, be seated," the pastor said, and we did.

Chapter 2

THE PASTOR STARTED his sermon about the prodigal son who returned, and how the father's love for him made him run toward him and how our father's love for us was the same.

Big enough to forgive all we have ever done.

I enjoyed the sermon and tried hard to listen while the pastor spoke, but someone sitting in front of me kept talking loudly. It was a young boy and a man whom I assumed was his father. I couldn't see their faces, but they were obviously quarreling, and their voices were growing louder.

"I knew you'd say that. Why can't you just tell me the truth for once," the boy said, hissing at his father.

"Keep it down," the man said.

A woman sitting next to them hushed them, and they went quiet for a few minutes until it started all over again. I was suddenly very pleased with my own daughter's behavior. We never yelled at each other that way. It's like they say; there's always someone who has it worse than you, right?

"What do you mean you can't trust me?" the man said, turning his head, looking at his son.

The boy scoffed loudly. "Don't give me that. You know perfectly well what I'm talking about."

The man shook his head and looked away. "I'm not having this discussion here. Not now."

That made the boy rise to his feet. "Yes, you are. I need to know, Dad. I deserve to know the truth. NOW! You've been lying to me all of my life! It ends here. Do you hear me? It ends HERE!"

"What on earth are you talking about?"

By yelling, the boy had attracted the attention of everyone in the church, even Pastor Johnson, who had stopped his preaching. He was looking down at them, a surprised look in his eyes, a look that seemed mostly concerned. He was only displaying what the rest of us were feeling—concerned and uncomfortable. Like spectators to a show we weren't invited to. This was clearly a discussion that wasn't meant to be had in church. It was the kind of thing that should stay behind closed doors.

"Sit down, son," the dad said, speaking through gritted teeth. "You're embarrassing me."

"No," the boy said, on the verge of tears now. "I am done doing what you tell me. I am done with you."

And with those words, he reached inside his hoodie and pulled out a gun. He held it between both hands, and it was shaking as he placed it against his father's head.

If he didn't before, then he most certainly had the church's attention now. A wave of panic rushed through the crowd, and someone yelled:

"Gun! He's got a gun!"

I felt Josie's hand on my arm as she raised her head.

"Dad?"

"Get down," I told her, and she ducked behind the pew, arms above her head.

The boy with the gun was shaking violently as he sobbed and pressed it against his father's temple. The father had raised his hands above his head and was tilting his head, trying to get away from the gun while whimpering lightly, his terrified eyes lingering on his son at the other end of the gun.

"Please, Nick."

"Don't do this," I said to the boy, approaching him. He didn't look at me. He stared down at his dad, his lips quivering.

"Stay out of this," he suddenly said to me. "You don't know anything."

"Then, let's talk," I said. "Tell me all about it. But don't ruin your life by doing this. If you pull that trigger, there's no going back. Your dad will die, you'll go to jail, and you'll have to live with the fact that you've killed someone for the rest of your life. And believe me; that's not something you'd wish for yourself."

"Yeah?" the boy said as he sniffled. "And just how do you know? You ever killed anyone?"

"As a matter of fact, I have," I said.

That made him turn his head and look at me.

"Really?"

I nodded, then pulled out my Miami PD badge. "One of the downsides to the job. It doesn't matter how bad these people are; it still haunts you for the rest of your life. Now, God will forgive you, but you'll never be able to forgive yourself. You'll always keep wondering if there wasn't some other way, always wish that you had done something different. It doesn't matter if the guy you killed is a murderer himself or even someone who has hurt children. They'll still visit you in your nightmares. The question is still there; couldn't it have ended differently? Did he have to die?"

The boy stared down at his father while the church was slowly being cleared out around us. People were running for their lives, storming out of the emergency exits, some were crying, others screaming. Nick didn't seem to care. He wasn't there to perform a mass shooting. His focus was solely on his dad.

"Nick," I said. "It might give you ten seconds of relief to shoot him because of whatever he has done to you, but it's not worth it. Trust me."

The boy glared down at his dad, the gun still shaking in his hands. I was sweating heavily, my heart pounding in my chest.

"Just give me the gun, Nick. Just hand it to me."

I could tell he was contemplating it; he was considering doing as I told him, at least for a few seconds. He lifted his head and looked at me, our eyes locking. I saw nothing but deep despair in them. The gun was lowered slightly, and he leaned over like he was about to do as I told him when there was movement from the other side. I turned to look as a local police officer entered. I had seen him outside the building when entering. Like all other churches in the area, they had a police officer guarding the entrance when we came and left, and sometimes they even had a car on the street and officers directing traffic outside.

"Drop the gun!" he yelled, holding his gun pointed at Nick. Seeing this, my heart dropped.

"Please," I said, lifting my badge. "He was about to hand it over to me."

But Nick was confused now. I reached out my hand and said to him. "Nick, just give me the gun. Please, before this officer finds it necessary to shoot."

Nick stared at me, then at the officer. The gun was no

longer at his father's temple, so the dad saw a chance to get away. He sprang forward, leaping for the end of the row. Seeing this, Nick gasped, then panicked. He turned around and fired a shot at him. This prompted the officer to fire as well, and a second later, I stood with Nick in my arms as I grabbed him when he fell, blood gushing out on my white, newly-ironed church shirt.

Chapter 3

IT HAD BEEN A PRETTY quiet day so far at the ER. Jean was working the morning shift and had just helped a little girl who had fallen off her bike. She had gotten a cast on her arm, and now Jean was handing her a lollipop for her braveness. That's when they got the message.

They were bringing in two victims of a gunfight.

After that, there was not a quiet moment. As soon as they were rushed in, Jean didn't sit down for the rest of her shift.

The young teenage boy was in the worst shape. His father, who had also been shot, had suffered a gunshot wound to his upper arm and was brought into surgery right away, where they managed to remove the bullet and patch him up. The bullet hadn't fractured any bones or hit any organs.

The young boy was a completely different story. He had suffered a gunshot to his chest, and they fought for his life in there for hours and hours. They had asked Jean to assist. It broke Jean's heart to see such a young man going through something like this at his age. He had his entire life ahead of him.

At least he was supposed to.

He had lost a lot of blood, and they brought in bag after bag of O-negative, while the doctors shook their heads, unsure how this was going to end. Dr. Harris, who Jean often worked with, had that look in his eyes that she didn't care much for, the one that told her he was close to giving up hope.

"We're losing him, Doctor," she told him as his blood pressure suddenly dropped rapidly. "Doctor?"

The sound of the heartrate flatlining was possibly the worst in the world, and as she heard it, Jean's heart knocked against her ribcage. She pulled out the defibrilla-tor, and the doctor resuscitated the boy's heart. The heart rate came back up, but only to flatline again. They did the same things all over again, and the same thing happened. The third time, they succeeded in keeping his heart pump-ing, and Jean breathed again for the first time in minutes.

She knew she wasn't supposed to get emotionally invested in patients, but it was hard not to, especially when it involved those whose lives you had fought for. She wanted this boy to live so badly; she almost cried when his heartrate flatlined again a few minutes later.

"Not today," Doctor Harris said and used the defibril-lator once again. "We're not losing you today."

The boy's body jolted as the electric shock went through him, and Jean turned to look at the monitor, praying for a heartbeat.

Come on; come on.

A second later, one came. And this time, it continued. Sweat sprang from her forehead as the doctors continued their work and were finally able to patch the boy up before he was taken to the ICU.

At the end of the day, she stood by his door, peeking inside and watching him. She then grabbed her purse and left the hospital, tears streaming across her cheeks. Not because she was sad, but because she loved her job so much. She loved being a part of saving lives. But at the same time, she hated how much bad stuff she had to witness every day. She hated that she lived in a world where young boys and their fathers got shot.

As she drove down her street, she saw a shadow on the porch of her neighboring house, and she breathed heavily. She parked the car and got out, then spotted Harry sitting on his swing.

Chapter 4

"HEY THERE, NEIGHBOR."

She wasn't supposed to since they were trying to stay away from one another, but something compelled her to walk up the stairs, up onto the porch where he was sitting. And as she saw his face, she realized why.

He had been crying.

"Are you okay? Harry?"

He shook his head, then bit his lip and leaned back in the swing. She sat down next to him, grabbing his hands between hers. His eyes were red-rimmed, and he didn't look at her.

"Oh, Harry. What's going on? What's happening? Is it Josie?"

He shook his head, then sniffled. He leaned his head against her shoulder. It was odd when a man as big as Harry, who was six-foot-eight and weighed around two hundred and thirty-something pounds, leaned against a small woman like Jean. It had to be an odd sight.

"Is it Camille? Is something wrong with Camille?"

He lifted his head and wiped his eyes. "I'm sorry. I'm just…"

She smiled. "Tell me, Harry. What happened?"

"There was this kid. In church. He was fighting with his father in the row in front of us. He then pulled out a gun. He wanted to shoot his dad but ended up getting shot himself. I was so close to helping him. He was so close to handing me the gun, and then…well, it all went wrong."

"I think I know who you're talking about," she said. "He was brought into the ER, and so was his dad."

"I am afraid to ask, but…"

Jean squeezed his hands. It killed her to sit there with him this close and not be able to kiss him ever again.

"He is alive, Harry. It was a close call, but he is still alive. The doctors say he has a good chance of recovery."

"Oh, God, that makes me so relieved to hear," he said. He chuckled, grabbed her face between his hands, leaned over, and placed a kiss on Jean's lips.

It took them both by surprise and, startled, they both pulled away. Jean rose to her feet and walked a few steps toward the stairs, her heart pounding in her chest.

What the heck?

"I'm…" Harry said. "I'm sorry, Jean. I was just so happy. I didn't think."

She shook her head. "You can't do that, Harry. You can't just kiss me and then regret it. It's not fair to me."

He got up. "And I don't want to. The fact is, I don't regret it at all. I want to be able to kiss you every day, Jean. I think I…"

"Don't you dare. Don't even think about going there," she said, raising her hand to stop him.

"But why not?" Harry lowered his voice. "I want to do the right thing, but the fact is, I'm not sure I love Camille anymore."

Jean shook her head. "I don't want to hear anymore, Harry."

"I could divorce her," he said.

"No!" Jean said. "Don't you even say that. Camille is not herself. She might get better with treatment, and then what? You're a family, remember? What about Josie?"

That made Harry stop, and she knew he hadn't thought any of it through. He was acting on impulse, and that wasn't good enough for Jean. She loved him, she truly did, and she'd give anything to be with him. But she couldn't be the one to break up a family, especially not when she loved his daughter and wife so dearly. She couldn't be that person. Plus, she knew Harry would never leave Camille when she was at her most vulnerable. It was never going to happen. It simply wasn't in his nature.

He stared at Jean, and she shook her head.

"I'll forget this even happened. I need to go to bed now. Go and be with your family. Goodnight, Harry."

Chapter 5

I WATCHED her walk down the stairs and toward her own house, cursing myself. I had blown it, hadn't I? We were doing so well, and now I had ruined everything. Why did I have to kiss her?

I had acted on impulse, and I hadn't thought about it. It was an accident, except it wasn't. Because accidents weren't something you usually really wanted to happen, were they? I wanted this to happen; I longed to kiss her so terribly.

The thing was, I felt more and more detached from Camille lately, especially since I felt like I hadn't even known her back before she overdosed. When I met her, she was a drug addict, and I helped her get clean, and we fell in love. But she had never told me much about herself. I barely knew anything about her childhood or her life before she met me. I had never met any members of her family or even friends. Her excuse was that they all lived in the Caribbean, in the Dominican Republic, and the only friends she had here in Miami were related to her drug abuse, so she didn't want anything to do with them. But I knew she went to FIT at one point; there had to be at least someone decent that she knew from back then, right?

I walked back inside and went into her room, where she was lying, staring at the ceiling. Josie was sitting in there, holding her mother's hand in hers.

"Are you okay?" I asked. "With everything that happened today. Must have been scary."

She sighed and nodded. "It was pretty scary. Mostly when the shots were fired. I thought they'd hit you."

I smiled. "So, you were worried about your old man, huh?"

She nodded. "I'm always worried about you."

I nodded pensively. Josie wasn't fond of the fact that I was a detective. She was terrified I'd get shot one day, and she'd lose me too. I couldn't blame her.

"I don't feel like she's getting any better," Josie said and looked at her mom. "Are you sure they know what they're doing at that rehabilitation center?"

"I'm pretty sure, yes. But I've recently heard of a different type of treatment that I am willing to try. They've had some pretty interesting results with cases like your mother's."

"Really?"

I nodded. "A nurse at the rehabilitation center told me about it and gave me a number. I'll call them tomorrow and see what they might be able to do for all of us."

"That sounds awesome, Dad." She looked at her mother, who was drifting in and out of sleep now.

Josie whispered, "I really miss her, you know?"

"I know," I said.

We stared at Camille in silence, each of us thinking about her when she had been herself…back when we had been a real family. I could hardly remember those days or what our relationship was like. Had I loved her? I knew I had. I just couldn't really find those emotions again. I kept wondering who wanted to kill her and why. Was it the people behind the trafficking ring? And did they still want her dead? There was so much I didn't understand, and maybe it was wrong of me, but it made me resent her. I couldn't help being angry with her for somehow putting Josie and me in this situation, for breaking our daughter's heart like this. If she had been involved with the wrong crowd and kept it a secret from me, I didn't know if I would be able to stay married to her.

"Why do you think he did it?" Josie suddenly asked, breaking my train of thought. She got up from her chair, and we walked out of Camille's room. Her breathing had gotten heavy, and we knew she was asleep.

"Who?" I asked, closing the door behind us.

"That kid. At church? Why do you think he pulled the gun on his father?"

"That's a very good question, honey."

"I mean, I know what it's like to be angry with my dad, but it takes a lot to go where he went…if you know what I mean."

I looked at my gorgeous daughter as she walked up the stairs to her room. The thought had crossed my mind too while thinking about what had happened earlier.

What would make a young teenage boy try to kill his own dad?

THREE WEEKS LATER

Chapter 6

I KNOCKED and opened the door to my boss's office.

"You wanted to see me?"

"Come in, Hunter," he said and signaled for me to enter. "Close the door behind you."

I did, then went to sit across from him. Fowler and I had known each other and worked together all of our adult lives. He was the one who climbed the career ladder while I remained on the floor and in the field. I preferred it this way as I was never cut out to be a leader. I'd rather be out there getting my fingers dirty. But that wasn't Fowler. He seemed to thrive being in this big office and carrying the weight that came with the title of Major.

"I need you to be careful out there, Hunter," he said, folding his hands on the desk, with serious eyes, his eyebrows furrowing.

"Me? I'm always careful," I said.

"Listen to me. You need to watch your back out there," he said and pointed at the door. "You're not exactly the most popular guy around here."

"I know," I said. "Not everyone likes what I've done,

seeing their colleagues go down like that. But I'm sure I'll be fine. It had to be done."

Fowler placed a small bag on the table, then slid it toward me. "I had someone I trust sweep my office. They found this. They bugged me, Harry. That's how they've stayed on top of things, staying out of trouble. That's also how they knew how to find Josie. You know when you thought you'd put her in a safe place with Al and told me about it, remember?"

Remember? How could I ever forget? My daughter had been kidnapped and almost murdered by my ex-colleague, Detective Ferdinand, before he ended up killing himself. He and several others from my precinct were all part of the human trafficking group, smuggling refugees into the country from Guatemala and the Caribbean. The case was still ongoing, and the FBI was working it with my cooperation. Right before he died, Ferdinand was also the one who had told me that Camille was somehow involved in all of it. I had wondered if Fowler had been in on it as well since he was the only one who knew where Josie was, and yet they found her anyway, but this little bag on the table explained everything. I could trust Fowler again, and that made me feel good. But it could also mean that there were still people around here that we couldn't trust… people that wanted us gone.

"I'll be all right," I said and reached over to grab the bag with the microphone. "Can I borrow this?"

"Be my guest," he said.

I looked at it in the light, then put it in my pocket. "The kid."

"What kid?"

"From the shooting at my church three weeks ago. What's gonna happen to him?"

"He's recovered," Fowler said. "He's in custody now. They're gonna try him as an adult."

"An adult? He's fifteen?" I said.

Fowler shrugged. "He brought a gun to church. He shot his own father. You know his dad is the State Attorney, right? They can't go easy on the boy. He knew what he was doing. He's old enough. Besides, that's not our department."

"Still. He's just a kid. One year older than my Josie. Is he talking? Has he explained anything?"

Fowler shook his head. "He won't say a word to anyone. Not even his lawyer."

I nodded. "Can I have a go at him?"

Fowler chuckled. "I wouldn't know why you'd want to."

"Just indulge me, will you? I think I connected with him at the church. I feel bad for him. At least give him the chance of telling his side of the story, right?"

"I will never learn to understand you, Hunter. But if you really want to, then knock yourself out. I'm not stopping you."

Chapter 7

THE TREATMENT CENTER was located in a three-story yellow building north of Miami. Doctor Kendrick, who was a small blonde woman with comforting eyes, greeted us in her office. I rolled Camille's chair inside and sat down.

"Okay," she said and looked at the papers I had brought her. It was Camille's medical file.

"As you can see, the doctors didn't think she'd ever wake up and become responsive again," I said. "But she did."

"And that was three months ago?" she asked, looking at Camille, whose eyes were on her as well. Her right arm had a couple of spasms, and she tried to speak, but it didn't make any sense.

"Yes. Approximately. Unfortunately, I don't think there has been much improvement over the past months, even though she goes to rehabilitation therapy three times a week. She does speak a few more words, and she does seem to be more responsive when I talk to her, but she can't control any of her movements, let alone do simple tasks like eating on her own."

"I see," Doctor Kendrick said.

"I don't know if I'm just being impatient or..." I said.

"It's only natural, Mr. Hunter," she interrupted me. "Once we begin to see progress in the ones we love, we expect things to move a lot faster than what they do. With that being said, I do think we can help her. Looking at her file, she seems to be a perfect fit for what we do here. Now, there are a few things I want to make sure you understand before we begin anything."

"Yes, of course."

"Now, treating Anoxic Brain Injury with hyperbaric treatment, in a hyperbaric chamber, is not FDA approved yet. We have research suggesting it works, and we have seen cases where it does work. Recently, we had a little girl who nearly drowned and had been dead for two hours, with no heartbeat and, therefore, no oxygen flowing to her brain. She was—like your wife here—unresponsive for months, till she came here. That doesn't mean it's some miracle treatment. There are doctors out there who will claim we were just lucky. That there is no evidence that it was due to our treatment. Now, since it is not FDA approved, your insurance won't pay."

I nodded. "I'm well aware of that. I'll pay out of pocket, even though it will drain my budget."

"Very well, Mr. Hunter," she said, smiling. "Now, the way the treatment works...what your wife has is Anoxic Brain Injury, as you are very well aware. It's a type of brain injury caused by oxygen deprivation. This can cause serious damage as the brain depends on oxygen to function properly. We know now that brain cells without oxygen will begin to die after only six minutes. There are several ways to suffer anoxic brain damage. Nearly drowning, experiencing a lack of oxygen due to a heart issue, or like in your wife's case, an overdose of drugs. Now the use of Hyperbaric Oxygen Therapy can promote healing by restoring oxygen levels and improving the flow of oxygen-rich blood to the brain. This can help blood vessels to grow and repair damaged tissue. The treatments are designed to help her injured brain cells shrink, expose healthy neurons, and 'wake them up' with pure oxygen. We provide oxygen to the patient in a pressurized chamber, giving her the same air pressure as air at sea level for forty-five minutes twice a day. Now, as I said, we can't promise you anything, but we have seen great results in other patients like her. Like the girl I talked about who is now functioning at almost a normal level for her age, which is quite remarkable."

I exhaled nervously. This was a big decision, one that I had to make all alone. "And what are the side effects?"

"She might feel slight discomfort in her ears because of the pressure, kind of like in an airplane. It can get very hot in the chamber while it's being pressurized, and she might feel fatigued, lightheaded, and hungry after the treatments. More severe complications can be lung damage, fluid buildup or rupture of the eardrum, sinus damage, and changes in vision causing nearsightedness, or myopia. There's the possibility of oxygen poisoning, which can cause lung failure, fluid in the lungs, or seizures. But side effects are normally mild as long as the therapy doesn't last more than two hours, and the pressure inside the chamber is less than three times that of the normal pressure in the atmosphere. Now, we will take her temperature and do a general health check before we begin the treatment, just to make sure she's in good health, that she doesn't have a cold or any respiratory issues. After that, we should be good to go."

I looked at Camille briefly, then exhaled. "I think we're

in. Right now, we'll take anything we can get if there is even a remote chance of improvement."

Chapter 8

I WORKED on my computer while Camille was in the chamber, receiving her first treatment. I was nervous as they slid the lid on top of her and closed the chamber. I could see her face through the small glass window in the chamber from where I was sitting, and she seemed comfortable enough. It was always hard to tell with her, and I worried that she was scared or maybe even in pain. But Doctor Kendrick, who was in the room with us the whole time, assured me that she was doing very well, that there was nothing to worry about.

Once she was done, they helped me put her back in her wheelchair, and I was told to be back the next day, early in the morning. They wanted us to come in every morning and every evening, so I was going to have to work my schedule around her treatments. It wasn't going to be easy, but if it provided any results, it would be worth it.

"How did it go? Is she any better?"

Josie was all over us as soon as we came through the front door. She looked at her mother, but as she saw no improvement, she gave me a disappointed look. Typically, the impatient teenager had expected an immediate response.

"She looks the same," she said.

"Josie, sweetie. It will take a while before we'll see any results," I said, then helped Camille get back into her room and lay her down on her bed. She was exhausted and fell asleep right away.

"But…" Josie said.

"We have to be patient," I said, grabbing her by the shoulders. "I have great confidence in the doctor and this treatment, and in God, naturally."

Josie sighed as we walked back into the kitchen, and I started dinner. I was making spaghetti and meatballs, and seeing this, Josie wrinkled her nose at the meat.

"So, how long do you think it'll take?" she asked.

I found an onion and started to cut it up, then exhaled tiredly. It had been a long day for me as well. I dreamt of lying on the couch and putting up my feet.

"I don't know, honey. To be honest, I need…"

I stopped when a foul smell hit my nostrils. Josie noticed it too.

"What's that smell?"

"It smells burnt," I said.

We both turned to look toward the front door, where something lit up the darkness outside by the windows leading to the porch.

"Stay here," I told her, then walked to the window and peeked out. Out on the front lawn, I spotted something that made me almost lose it.

"What is it, Dad? Dad?"

"Stay here!"

I hurried back into the kitchen, grabbed the fire extinguisher, then ran to the door and pulled it open. I rushed down the stairs into the front yard, where someone had put my trash bins and set them on fire. I ran down there, opened the extinguisher, and put it out, covering everything in the white foam. The smoke hit my face, and it smelled awful, so I turned away.

As I did, I saw a word written in red paint on my garage door. The letters were covering the entire surface, making them as tall as I was. The paint was still wet and running, but the message was clear enough:

RAT

Chapter 9

"WHAT WAS THAT?"

Josie stared at me as I hurried inside and closed the door behind me. "Why were our trash bins on fire?"

"It was nothing," I lied. I didn't want her to worry. I closed the door to make sure she didn't go outside and see the writing.

"It looked like something, Dad."

"It was just kids, okay? Pranks, you know."

She calmed down. "Oh, okay."

I smiled, then continued my cooking, shaping the meatballs. Josie stayed with me for a few minutes more, seeming like she wanted to talk, but then eventually giving up.

"I have homework," she said, then walked upstairs. "Call me when dinner is ready."

Normally, at a moment like this, I would have told her to help me set the table, but not this time, not today. As soon as she was gone up the stairs, I grabbed a bucket of soap and water, then ran out to the garage door and started to wash off the paint, scrubbing it. I got most of it off and was about to walk back inside when Jean came up behind me.

"What's going on?"

I turned to look at her, my heart jumping at the sight of her.

"What's this?"

"Someone set our trash bins on fire and wrote RAT on my garage door. I think they're trying to scare me off from talking to the feds."

She nodded. "The trafficking case, huh. So, you think it might be your colleagues who did this?"

I shrugged. "Could be. I'm not exactly popular around the station for doing what I'm doing. But they don't scare me. I will not stop till all of them are brought to justice, that's for sure."

Jean smiled and nodded. "I wouldn't expect any less from you. But what about Josie?"

"What about her?"

Jean pointed toward the burned-out bins in my front yard. The smell of melted plastic was still thick.

"Did she see this?"

"She saw the fire, but not the writing. I told her it was a prank. I'm not sure she believed me. She's getting too smart for me. I just don't want her to worry about this too. She has enough with her mother and all. She even says she's constantly worried about me getting hurt or killed while at work. It's too much for such a young girl. She should be worrying about her friends and boys and stuff like that."

"So, what are you going to do about this?" Jean asked.

I shook my head, then poured the last soapy water on the garage door. I had managed to wash away most of it, even though you still could see the trace of what had been written.

"Ignore them. That's what you do with bullies."

Chapter 10

THE PRE-TRIAL DETENTION center was located right across the street from the Richard E. Gerstein Justice Building on 13th Street. A handful of security guards in green jackets stood outside the entrance to both buildings as I drove through the gates and into the detention center, known to be one of the toughest in the nation. In there were the most hardcore criminals, awaiting their trials.

And then there was Nick. Fifteen-year-old Nick Taylor.

I was shown into a room with benches and tables that were bolted to the floor, so they couldn't be moved or lifted in the air and used as weapons.

Nick entered, heavily chained on his hands and feet, then sat down across from me while the guard stood only a few feet away. I tried to smile, but it was hard to be sincere in these circumstances. The boy had lost a lot of weight since I had last seen him in the church, and he was paler than the barren white walls behind him.

"Nick?" I said, trying to look into his eyes, but he kept staring at the floor beneath him.

"My name is Harry Hunter. I'm a detective with Miami PD, and I've come here to help you."

No reaction. I hadn't expected one, but it didn't make it less uncomfortable.

"I was there when you pulled the gun out. I was sitting right behind you. Maybe you remember me? I tried to persuade you to hand me the gun. I was the one who tried to tell you not to ruin your life. Do you remember, Nick?"

No reaction. I tried another approach.

"I want to help you, Nick. They want to try you as an adult, and you're looking at some serious charges here. If you tell someone why you did it, then maybe we could be…"

I stopped myself. I didn't know if telling his story would actually help him or not. The fact was, he had attempted to kill his father, and in a public place on top of it, where he risked the lives of many others. The media was all over his story—the State Attorney's son being tried for attempted murder. They had practically already convicted him. I was no attorney. I couldn't promise him anything. I saw him do it, so there was no doubt of his guilt. But I could be there for him; I could listen to his story.

"I've read up on your background, Nick," I said and found his file. I placed it on the table, then opened it. "Your mother, she died ten years ago, didn't she?"

Still, no answer.

"It says here she disappeared on a road trip to Key West ten years ago. Her body was discovered three days later in the water down there, hidden underneath the mangroves. A fisherman spotted her, it says here."

The boy remained still even though he was now fiddling with a loose string on his orange jumpsuit. I couldn't tell if he was reacting at all to what I was saying.

My guess was that he was hurting too badly even to be able to look at me.

"What did he do to you, Nick?" I asked, closing the file with a deep exhale. "See, I don't believe a boy like you did this without a valid reason. I think your father did something to make you do this." I slammed my palm onto the metal table between us. The sound was louder than I had intended it to be and bounced off the walls.

"What did he do to make you so mad? Come on, talk to me."

That's when I finally got my reaction. Nick lifted his eyes and looked into mine while I continued, "The way I see it, you had enough. You got angry, maybe you were even scared of him, and that's why you pulled the gun. And you might not want to tell me or anyone why, but I'm not letting him get away with it, you hear me?"

The guard signaled for me that my time was up and went to grab Nick. He stared at me, his green eyes piercing through me. Then as he rose to his feet, he finally spoke while being pulled away, "I remember you, Detective. I remember you."

Chapter 11

"I THINK he was about to talk just when they took him away."

My dad looked at me. We were sitting at the dinner table and had just finished our pizza. I had been to late afternoon therapy with Camille, and Josie was in her room doing her homework.

"And what did he say?" My dad asked and grabbed another slice of pizza, even though he had stopped eating minutes ago. My dad was very fond of food in general, especially the unhealthy kind.

"He said he remembered me," I said. "From the day he shot his dad, he remembered me. I made a connection with him, which no one else has been able to do."

My dad chewed and swallowed. He washed it down with iced tea. "So, what will you do next?"

"I'm gonna go back in a couple of days and see him again," I said. "Maybe he'll finally open up to me and talk then; maybe I can get the whole story. I don't feel good about this case, especially not about the father. Something is off, and the boy is the one taking the fall."

"So, you believe the father might have hurt the kid, is that it?"

I leaned back with a deep sigh. "Maybe. In my book, it takes a lot for a fifteen-year-old to try and kill his own dad. And I remember he said stuff to him before he pulled the gun out."

"What stuff?"

"Like he had been lying to him all of his life, that he was done trusting him. Something like that," I said and sipped my own iced tea.

"So, you believe it has to do with his mother's death, am I right?"

I exhaled and drank again. "Yes. Of course, I do."

"Did they suspect foul play in her death?" he asked, reaching over for yet another slice and biting into it. My dad had gained a lot of weight in the years since my mom died. She was the one who reminded him to stop eating and to exercise. He kept himself fit for her sake, but now that she wasn't here anymore, he had let himself go. I wondered if I should say something. I decided not to. He was in his seventies and didn't have to look good for anyone. He could have his pizza and enjoy it if he liked. I just wanted him to live long and stay with us for many years and not develop heart issues or anything like that.

"They concluded that she drowned, but the case was never closed. I found it when looking around a little and had the files sent up here from the Key West archives. Kate Taylor and two of her best friends were on a road trip to Key West. According to these women, it was Kate's thirty-fifth birthday, and she wanted to spend it with her friends, partying in Key West and then go swimming with dolphins in Key Largo. But they only made it to Key West. They partied that night, and she was seen dancing with some guy—they searched for him for a long time. All they knew was that his name was Matt and that he was tall and had brown hair and blue eyes. That's it. The girl's friends reported her missing the next day when she didn't come back to the hotel. At first, they thought she was out with this guy, and that she'd come back eventually, but when she didn't, they went to the police. The police searched for her for several days, and three days later, a fisherman found her floating in the shallow water, hidden under the mangroves. They concluded she had died from drowning. Maybe she went swimming at nighttime and got in trouble."

"But the case was never closed, you say?"

"No. They kept looking for this Matt guy, thinking he might be able to shed light on how a very good swimmer like Kate could suddenly drown. Was she pushed in? Did she fall from a boat? She had no bruises on her body, so there was no sign of being forced. So, what happened? It ends there."

My dad nodded pensively. "So, you think the dad might have killed her? The Miami-Dade County State Attorney?"

I shrugged. "She was away without him, dancing with another man. He could have followed her there; he could have gotten jealous, who knows?"

"You think Nick knows, don't you?"

I nodded. "It would explain a lot, wouldn't it?"

Chapter 12

I WAS RUNNING LATE for Camille's afternoon appointment and rushed in through the doors, pushing her wheelchair ahead of me.

It had been two weeks since we started coming to the treatment center, and I was finding it increasingly more and more difficult to be everywhere I was needed. Josie was complaining because I was never at home anymore, while Fowler was complaining because I didn't show up in time for morning briefings, even though I had told him I had to be at the treatment center every morning at nine and every afternoon at five. My cases were being neglected as I seemed to be trying to be several places at once, ending up being nowhere. At least, that's how it felt. When I was at work, my mind was constantly at home, thinking about all the stuff I needed to do, all the laundry I hadn't done, all the dishes in the sink, and the dental appointments for Josie, along with her volleyball games and practices, trying to figure out how I was supposed to drive her there while going to the treatment center with her mother.

On top of it all, I had to remember to make a lunch for Josie every day and figure out what to cook for dinner.

It was a lot to balance at once.

While Camille received her treatment in the hyperbaric chamber, most of my thoughts were with Nick Taylor. I had been going through the old case files of his mother's death again and again and read every article that was ever written about her disappearance, and every time, it came down to the mysterious Matt. The guy she had been with on the night she died. No one seemed to know who he was or had even seen him when the police asked them back then. Not even the bartender at Sloppy Joe's, where they were drinking and dancing, could remember him. It was just the two friends.

Or was it?

While Camille was inside her chamber, I suddenly realized something. I flipped a couple of pages in the case files until I reached the two statements taken by the police—the first interviews with Kate Taylor's two friends, Joan and Kristin. There was something about them that had rubbed me the wrong way from the beginning when I first read through them.

They weren't a match. And in the places they were a match, they were too much of a match, too similar, down to the choice of words. I didn't like how they both said that she was *bummed out about her marriage* and that she needed to *blow off some steam*, and she *wished she could just disappear*. They were some very distinct sentences and sounded almost rehearsed…like they had memorized them. And then there was the thing about the guy, Matt. Only the first woman, Kristin, spoke about him on her own. She talked about him like he had been there all evening and said that Kate was *all over him*—that she was crazy about him. Whereas her other friend Joan didn't even remember him when asked, or maybe she didn't want to mention him? Could she be covering for him? Did she know him? While Kristin described him as tall, brown hair and blue eyes, Joan called him bald and stated that she couldn't really remember him and that she didn't believe that Kate was very interested in him and that she wouldn't cheat on her husband. Meanwhile, according to Kristin, she would definitely be able to cheat on her husband.

It didn't match up.

Who was telling the truth?

Was Joan lying to protect this guy?

I leaned back, running a hand through my hair, wondering about this and why they hadn't looked more deeply into this ten years ago, when Doctor Kendrick came in, smiling. Her blonde hair was in a ponytail today, and it made her look younger. Her brown eyes smiled at me.

"I think she's done for today. You ready to take her home?"

Chapter 13

I DROVE up in front of my house, my mind still occupied by Kate Taylor's death, going through the many possibilities, always returning to the one theory I couldn't escape: That Andrew Taylor, Kate's husband and Nick's father, killed her in a fit of jealous rage, angry that she spent the night with some other guy, dancing and maybe even sleeping with him on her thirty-fifth birthday, and that Joan somehow knew this Matt guy and wanted to protect him.

I turned off the engine with a deep sigh, then got out and grabbed the wheelchair from the back and rolled it up to the door, then opened it and looked in at Camille. Usually, she would be half asleep at this point, tired from her treatment, but not today. Today, she looked at me and smiled, almost laughed as I peeked inside to help her out. Seeing this and hearing her light laughter, I couldn't help laughing too.

"What's so funny?" I asked. "Was it something I said?"

Knowing she couldn't answer, I bent over to get her seatbelt off, but as I did, she reached out her hand and grabbed mine. With a light gasp, I lifted my head and looked into her eyes. She was smiling widely while we were holding hands, lifting them in the air. It was a coordinated maneuver that I knew she hadn't been able to do before. Our eyes locked, and then she spoke, "Th-Thank…you."

I almost lost it at this moment. Until now, she hadn't been able to utter more than one word, and usually, it would make no sense and be completely out of context. Like when she told me someone had tried to kill her, she simply yelled out our daughter's name. This was different. This was her actually speaking to me.

"What did you say?" I asked, my eyes watering.

"Thank…you," she repeated, then much to my surprise, she continued: "For…for all you h-have done. I don't deserve it."

The words spoken were so clear and flowed from her mouth like it was barely difficult at all. Tears sprang to my eyes as I stared at her, still while we were holding hands and she moved hers in a coordinated fashion, pulling both of our hands up and down.

"I…I don't know what to say. Camille. The hand…the movements…and you're speaking!"

I said it while almost squealing. She smiled and nodded, tears spilling onto her cheeks.

"It's working," I said, shaking my head in disbelief. "I can't believe it. The treatments. They're really working!"

She nodded again while crying.

I lifted my head, then grabbed her head between my hands and looked into her eyes.

"You're back, Camille."

She lifted her hand and touched my cheek, then wiped away a tear that had escaped my eyes and rolled down my cheeks. The movement was small and seemingly insignificant, but not to me. To me, it was bigger than any moonwalk. I grabbed her hands and pulled her out of her seat, then stood with her in my arms for a few seconds, letting her stand on her feet; then, once I sensed she had balance, I let go. She stood for a few seconds, staring at me like I had abandoned her, but then realized she was standing on her own, actually standing on her own two feet. She wasn't leaning on the car, and not on me either.

I nodded, then reached out my hands.

"Come."

Camille took one step toward me, then another before she fell forward into my arms, her legs deflating beneath her due to the lack of muscles after years of not being used while she was stuck in a bed and chair.

I grabbed her, placed her in her chair, grinning so loudly that Josie must have heard it inside the house because she came running out onto the porch.

"Dad? What's going on?"

"Your mom," I yelled as I helped Camille sit in her chair. "She...she walked! She actually stood and then walked two steps toward me on her own."

Josie shrieked and ran down the stairs toward us.

"Really? She did?"

I couldn't hold back my tears as Josie threw herself into her mother's arms. Camille chuckled and cried at the same time, while Josie held her close.

"And she spoke," I said, wiping tears away from my cheeks. "She spoke real sentences, several of them."

"Really?" Josie said and looked at her mother. "Is this true? You're better now, like really better?"

Camille nodded. "I...am."

Chapter 14

JEAN WAS SITTING in her kitchen, eating Ramen noodle soup since she wasn't in the mood for cooking. She hadn't been for quite a while now, probably ever since she stopped cooking for Harry and his family. It was like it was pointless now that it was just herself and not an entire family who needed her.

She missed being needed.

Jean sighed and looked into her soup. A lot seemed pointless these days. She was staying away from Harry, giving him his space and letting them be a family, but what did that mean for her? Where did that leave her?

Destined to be alone for the rest of her life?

You fell in love with the wrong guy.

That's what her mother would have said if she ever told her about him, which she never would. Her mother could be very judgmental when she wanted to, and she wanted to…a lot. It was like she enjoyed watching Jean lose confidence and feel like a child again. It was one of the reasons Jean never involved her in anything in her life.

She kept her mother at a distance so she wouldn't be able to criticize her for her choices in life.

But this one, she would have been right about. You blew it, Jean. You wasted your love on a man that wasn't available.

She had barely finished the thought, feeling sorry for herself, when she heard the screaming from outside in the street. It made her rush to the window and look out. There they were, Josie, Harry, and Camille.

Jean walked out on the porch, then looked down at them. As she stood there, Harry spotted her and called out to her.

"Jean! It's amazing!"

Jean walked down the stairs and approached them, heart pounding in her chest like a hammer.

"She walked," Harry said as Jean came close. He had tears in his eyes and his voice was breaking.

"And talked," Josie added. "God is healing her. God is so good!"

"He sure is. Isn't it wonderful?" Harry asked.

Jean looked at him. She wanted to scream. Of course, it was wonderful. Of course, it was a miracle and worth celebrating.

But it also shut down her hope of ever being with Harry, of him ever putting Camille in a home. If Camille was really coming back, Jean didn't stand a chance. She knew it was selfish to think like this since she should be thrilled for them, and in a way, she was. She just wasn't thrilled for herself, for her own sake.

She was devastated.

Jean forced a smile through her tears. "That is wonderful news, Harry, really. I am so happy for y'all."

"It's the new treatment," Harry said. "I've seen little improvements every time we've gone. Like her being more alert, her looking at me more when I spoke, and smiling more. Little things. And today, she took a huge leap forward. I have to say it was hard to believe that there would ever be any improvement. But here we are. I can't believe it, Jean."

Jean swallowed and nodded while looking into his sweet eyes, the very eyes she loved so dearly. She felt her eyes tear up and bit her lip.

"I should...I have to get back. But congratulations to all of you. It's amazing; it truly is."

While still speaking the last few words, Jean turned around and hurried toward her home. She walked up the stairs, then turned to look at them. As they rolled Camille back into the house, she made her decision.

It was time to move on.

Chapter 15

"THANK YOU, God, for bringing Camille back to us. We pray we'll continue to see improvement in her and that she'll recover completely. We know you can and will do it because you love us so much. Amen."

"Amen," Josie repeated.

She was lying in her bed, PJs on, and I realized that she had grown out of them again. We'd had a nice evening together, eating pizza again. Camille had lasted for only about half an hour before her head started to slump and I had to put her to bed. Before she dozed off, she looked at me, then grabbed my wrist.

"I…am…sorry," she said.

I shushed her. "You need to sleep."

She had dozed off before I finished the sentence, and I had watched her sleep for a few minutes, wondering what the coming days and weeks would bring. Would I finally get some answers? Would I finally get to know what really happened to her and how it was all connected?

Would she tell me the truth?

Would I like what she told me?

Would I love her again?

It was hard to tell. I knew I would go far for Josie's sake. I just didn't know how far I was willing to go.

"Good night, Daddy," Josie said as I turned out the lights and left her room.

"Good night, sweetie."

I closed the door and walked back into my own bedroom. I brushed my teeth and got out of my clothes. I liked to sleep in my boxers as I was usually very hot at night, so I ducked in under the covers and turned the lights off. Then I just laid there in the darkness while a million thoughts rushed through my mind. I was excited and frightened at the same time. It was a strange sensation. Was I ready for this? Was I ready to get Camille back even if it meant I got to know the truth about her? Could I handle the consequences?

I believed so.

I sighed and thought about Jean. I had been so excited earlier; I hadn't even stopped for a second to think about how she felt about it. It had to be tough on her, even though she pretended to be happy for our sake.

The thought made me feel terrible.

No matter what I did, no matter how this ended, someone's heart was going to be broken.

I closed my eyes and tried to sleep, willing myself to think about something else. But then Nick Taylor showed up, and I couldn't help feeling disillusioned. He didn't belong in with the adults, among the most dangerous criminals in this country.

If only I could find the connection. If only I could get him to tell me what made him so angry at his dad.

I got up and opened my laptop, then logged into the police database, searching for the boy's name. Something came up that I hadn't seen before, and suddenly I was looking at what might be exactly what I was searching for. At least it was a step in the right direction.

If only I knew where it led.

I closed the lid of the computer, then looked at the clock. It was almost three a.m., and I had been at it for hours. I turned off the light and was about to turn back in when I heard a bump from downstairs and my heart stopped.

Chapter 16

I GRABBED MY GUN, then walked into the hallway, holding it out in front of me. I walked to Josie's door, then peeked inside. She was sleeping soundly, so it wasn't her bumping around.

Another sound followed…footsteps across the wood.

Someone was down there.

I walked down the first few steps of the stairs, then paused to listen. When there was no sound, I took another few steps down, holding out the gun in front of me.

I reached the living room, then scanned the area quickly with my gun held out, but couldn't see anyone. I walked to the light switch and flipped it, then looked at the wall behind the couch.

Three big letters were painted in red. The paint was wet and still running, spelling one word:

RAT

Anger rose inside me, indescribable, uncontrollable anger. It was one thing that they wrote this on my garage door and set a trash bin on fire outside. But entering my home? My house? My sacred place, where my family and I believed we were safe?

That was something completely different.

I heard another noise, then turned to look. I found myself face to face with a man. He was wearing a black ski mask, and I couldn't see his eyes. He was standing by the door to Camille's room, holding a gun in his hand.

I pointed my gun at him.

"Hold it right there."

The man lifted his gun as well, and that was when I noticed. As he moved his jacket, attached to his belt, I saw a golden badge that looked very similar to mine.

He was a cop.

Realizing this, I lowered my gun slightly, then tried to look into his eyes, but he was too far away, standing in the darkness by her door.

"Who are you? What are you doing in my house?" I yelled and walked forward, letting my anger drive me. "Why have you come here?"

"Stop talking," the voice said. I didn't recognize it. He had to be from another department. "Stop talking to the feds, or you're a dead man."

"Says who?" I said, still approaching him, hoping to see his eyes better if I got a little closer. "Who are you, and why are you threatening me, huh? You think I'm scared of you, huh?"

"You're a dead man, Hunter," he said, lifting his gun. "We'll take your entire family if you don't shut up."

The mention of my family angered me further, and my finger on the trigger was hard to control. If I shot this guy now, I would have the law on my side. He was in my house, threatening me and my family.

"I'm not scared of you. Who do you work for?" I asked. "Who is behind all this?"

The guy looked at me, then backed up, turned around, and ran down the hallway. I was after him right away, springing toward him, grabbing him by the jacket and pulling him back. Just as I was about to pull the mask off, he reached up and punched me hard on the nose. I fell backward, still holding him, but he had the upper hand now, and the punches were falling on me, hard. This guy knew how to fight. I grabbed him in an armlock, holding him tight when a gun went off.

Chapter 17

JEAN WOKE UP WITH A START. She was gasping for air, heart pounding, and sweat springing to her forehead.

What was that? It sounded like a shot!

"Harry!"

She jumped out of her bed and stormed out the door, down the stairs and hurried toward Harry's house, heart in her throat.

Please, don't let them be hurt. Please, let them be all right.

She rushed up the stairs, grabbed the door handle, and tried to push it open, but it was locked.

"Shoot!"

Jean hurried back down the stairs to the front lawn and found the key inside the sprinkler that didn't work, where Harry kept it under the loose lid in case of emergency. Then she ran back up on the porch and unlocked the door.

She stormed inside.

"Harry? Josie?"

She almost screamed their names, worried sick. Someone appeared at the top of the stairs.

It was Josie.

"Josie," Jean said. "Are you okay? I heard a noise. What happened?"

She looked as confused as Jean felt. "I…I don't know. I woke up. There was a loud noise. Was it a shot I heard?"

"I don't know. I heard it too. Is your dad okay?" Jean asked, panting and agitated. "Is he all right?"

"I don't know," Josie said. "I don't even know where he is. He's not in his room. The door is open, and I can't see him in there."

Jean scanned the living room. The lights were on.

"Harry?"

Josie came down the stairs toward her.

"Da-a-a-d?"

Her voice was trembling. Jean struggled to keep calm, as well. She stared at the big red letters on the wall.

"Harry?"

Josie stood in front of her, staring up at the tall red letters, her hands shaking.

"W-what is this?" she asked. "Jean? What does this mean? Who did this? Who painted this?"

"I don't know," Jean said, then looked toward the hallway leading to Camille's room, where the door was left ajar.

"Harry?" she asked, then walked toward it, her hands shaking. If someone had broken into the house and hurt Harry, they could still be here; they could still be here, hiding out.

As she approached the hallway, Jean saw blood on the wooden floors. A trail of blood led away from Camille's room toward the back entrance. Jean paused and stared down at it, heart pounding in her chest.

What happened here?

"Harry?"

She pushed the door open with a shaking hand. Inside

Camille's room, she saw someone. He was sitting in a chair next to Camille's bed. Harry was only in his boxers, bent over Camille, his fists clenched. He had blood on his chin and chest.

"H-harry?"

He lifted his glance, and their eyes met.

"A-are you okay? We heard a noise, and it sounded like a shot being fired…?"

He nodded. "I shot him. By accident."

"Who did you shoot, Harry?"

"The intruder. We fought; the gun went off by accident. I think he was shot in the leg. Probably just a graze since the bullet was lodged in the wall."

"So…where is he now?"

"He escaped. When the shot went off, he punched me hard, and I blacked out for a few seconds. When I came to, he was gone. I hurried in here to make sure Camille was okay. She took an Ambien before she went to bed. She couldn't find rest, so I gave her one. Luckily, I think she slept through it all."

Jean approached him, then bent down. Her eyes filling, Jean bit her lip and leaned her forehead against Harry's, holding a hand behind his neck.

"I was so scared," she whispered. "I thought I lost you."

He closed his eyes and exhaled. His breath felt warm on her skin. His soft lips moved closer. She could feel them brush against hers.

"Dad?"

Josie showed up in the doorway, and Jean let go of Harry and pulled away with a light gasp. Josie stared at them, her eyes concerned and confused. Whether it was the blood on her father's body or because she had seen Jean and Harry in an intimate moment, Jean didn't know.

"Dad?"

He smiled. "I'm fine, Josie."

"You don't look fine."

"Well, you should have seen the other guy," he chuckled, trying to sound cheerful for his daughter.

"You're not hurt?" Jean asked. "Nothing I need to patch up?"

He shook his head. "Couple of bruises, but I'll be fine. I'll be sore tomorrow, but nothing else."

"You sure I shouldn't che…"

"Hello?" a voice sounded from the front door. "Hunter? You here?"

Harry lifted his gaze.

"That'll be Fowler," he said and got up.

"You called Fowler? You didn't call the police?" Jean asked, concerned. What was going on here? What was he not telling her?

"He is the police," Harry said, walking past her. "He's the only police I trust right now."

Chapter 18

"YOU DIDN'T GET to see his face or eyes at all?"

Fowler looked at me across the living room. I had sat down on my couch, Fowler in my recliner. He was scribbling notes on his pad. Up until now, I had been reasonably collected, but now that I was telling him everything that had happened, it was getting harder to keep my anger at bay.

I shook my head.

"He wore a ski mask. I was never close enough to see his eyes. I didn't recognize his voice."

"But you're certain he was one of ours?"

I nodded with a sniffle. Jean and Josie were in the kitchen, where Jean had served Josie some ice cream. They were both eating it, sitting at the breakfast counter, chatting. Every now and then, she'd throw me a glance, and our eyes would meet. She was trying to calm Josie down and make her think about something else, and I was very grateful for that.

"He had a badge, Fowler."

Fowler glared at the red letters on the wall, shaking his head. "I told you to watch your back."

"This was in my home," I said. "They were in my house, Fowler. In my own darn house!"

He lifted his hand. "I know. I know. We'll get them. And he was shot in the leg, you say?"

I nodded. "In the thigh, I'm pretty sure. It all went by a little fast."

"So, we'll call all the hospitals and see if they got anyone in tonight with a gunshot wound."

I exhaled and leaned back, closing my eyes. "It was just a graze, or he wouldn't have been able to run out of here. I can't believe they would go this far. I can't believe he was inside my house."

"How did he get in here?" Fowler asked. "Front door was locked, right? When Jean got here, she said it was still locked."

"Back door," I said. "It's been broken up. It's old, and one kick or even a mild push would have opened it."

"Might wanna get that fixed," he said.

I lifted my gaze and looked at him. "You think they'll be back?"

"I don't think they'll leave you alone till you stop talking, no. It's a dangerous game you're playing."

"But I can't back down now," I said. "These people are bad seeds; there's nothing worse than a corrupt cop. You have to agree with me on this. I have to clean up this mess."

He gave me another look. "Even if it means risking your family getting hurt? Because I have to tell you. I don't know what you're up against here, but it seems like they're willing to take it as far as they can. They're not backing down as long as you're not. Maybe you should consider backing off. I'm sure the FBI can run the case without you talking."

I wrinkled my forehead, then rose to my feet.

"How can you even suggest that?"

"I'm just worried about you, that's all," he said and rose to his feet as well. "I don't want you or your family hurt. You're risking losing everything, and I want to make sure it's worth it."

I shook my head in disbelief. "They're not gonna break me. I am not letting them win."

He threw out his hands. "All right, Hunter. The choice is yours. I'll make the calls and see if we can locate the cop who was in your house tonight and got himself shot. Until then, please be careful, will you? Stay alive for me. And get some sleep. You look terrible."

"Thanks," I said, smiling while letting him out. "I mean it."

Chapter 19

I PARKED the motorcycle in the alley and walked up to the backdoor of Al's building. She had moved locations since she recently had been attacked in her home, when I decided to hide Josie at her place, thinking she'd be safe there. She had only moved a few blocks further south, to a location just as remote as the former and even harder to find. It was the next morning after a night with next to no sleep. I had driven through town to get to her first thing.

Al was a former CIA hacker and the only one who could help me out. She was also slightly paranoid and kept herself hidden. From what, exactly, she had never told me, and I wasn't sure I wanted to know.

"Yes?" she asked over the intercom.

"It's Harry," I said.

"I can see that, you fool; there's a camera in this thing," Al said dryly. "What do you want?"

"Just let me in, will you?" I said.

"Last time I did, my place ended up like a warzone. Not only was I knocked out, but I was also compromised and had to move because of it. I want to make sure it won't happen again."

"I need your help," I said with a deep sigh. "I can't tell you the details in the street. Someone might hear me, and where will that leave us?"

"Okay. You make a valid point. Are you sure you're alone? Did anyone follow you here?" she asked.

"No. I'm sure I'm all alone," I said, yet still looked around me to be certain. It was more of a reflex than because I believed there would actually be someone there. "I rode here on my bike and took a couple of detours before I ran around the block three times until I was certain no one was following me. Just like you have instructed me to."

"And you're not bringing trouble my way?"

"That, I can't promise you. You know I can't," I said.

"At least you're honest," she said, then buzzed me in.

"Finally," I mumbled, and pushed the heavy door open, then rushed up the four flights of stairs. I knocked on the door and heard Al fumble with the many locks behind it before it was pulled open, and she peeked out through the crack.

"It's still me, Al."

"Just checking," she said, then opened the chain and the door and let me in before she closed it behind me and locked it thoroughly.

"Okay, you're in. What's up?"

I walked to her desk and wondered if she had gotten a few new monitors since I was last there. I counted at least three new ones. On one of them, it showed a place where it snowed, and people wore furry hats. I wondered if she was spying on some Russians. On another, they were all wearing masks inside of a supermarket, and I realized it had to be somewhere in Asia, maybe even China, where they had the outbreak of the Coronavirus. It had gotten pretty bad over the past few weeks, and the sale of masks had exploded even here in the States.

"I need you to take a look at this," I said and pulled out a small bag from my pocket. Inside it was the small device that Fowler had handed me in his office.

Al grabbed the bag and stared at it between her hands, studying it. "A microphone?"

"I need to know who owns this. Who installed it? I don't know how, but I thought maybe you could track it down somehow."

She stared at the small device, then nodded.

"I can do that."

Al emptied the bag and poured the microphone onto her desk, then picked it up with a pair of tweezers.

"Small one," she said. "A newer model. It's amazing how small they make them now, huh? Not much bigger than a pin. This looks like a pretty advanced model, though. This is not a cheap piece of equipment."

"That's what I was thinking," I said. "It's not something everyone can get their hands on."

"I'll look into it," she said, furrowing her brows beneath the dreadlocks while turning the device in the light.

"How's the family? How's Josie?"

I lifted my eyebrows. "You're asking about my daughter now? You never cared much before?"

She shrugged. "Well, you might say I feel closer to her these days. After what happened."

That made me smile. Al was far from as cold-hearted and uncaring as she liked to pretend to be.

"Josie's good," I said. "She's okay."

"And her heart?"

"No problems there. Her body seems to be accepting it well, and she's back in school."

Al looked at me, smiling wryly. "So, everything is back to normal? Then how come you didn't sleep last night?"

"Are you spying on me too?" I asked.

"No, you fool, I took one look at that face and knew. You have like no color in your cheeks."

"Ah, I see. Well, let's just say whoever put that microphone up has it in for me. They tried to attack us last night in our house."

"And I'm guessing it's all connected to what happened last month, to Josie's kidnapping and the refugees being smuggled in the appliances."

I wrinkled my forehead. "I never told you about that."

She smiled. "You don't have to. I have my ways."

"I know you do. That's why I'm bringing this to you. Not a word to anyone."

She lifted her eyebrows. "I never speak to anyone for that same reason. Except for you who keeps knocking on my darn door. Now, get out of here and let me work. I'll let you know when I have something."

Chapter 20

MY FINGER WAS SHAKING a little as I rang the doorbell. Not because I was nervous, but because of the many cups of coffee I had practically inhaled before I left the station. I had kept to myself all day while working, trying not to talk to anyone except Fowler in his office. Yet, I still couldn't help but see suspicious behavior everywhere and felt like all eyes were constantly on me. I kept listening in on conversations between my colleagues, trying to figure out if I recognized the voice from the night before. I was becoming paranoid, and it was about to drive me nuts.

I could hear someone coming down the stairs inside. The footsteps paused for a few seconds before they continued the rest of the way to the door.

A set of blue eyes landed on me as it swung open.

"Yes?"

"Kristin Holmes?"

She smiled politely. She had pretty eyes that looked up at me with wonder, reminding me of a child.

"It's Grant now," she said. "I took my husband's name when we married last summer. How can I help you?"

I showed her my badge. "Harry Hunter, Miami PD. I wondered if we could have a little chat?"

Seeing the badge made her eyes begin to flicker, and she was suddenly slightly flustered. It wasn't an unusual reaction when I came to people's homes like this. They all worried if they could have done something wrong.

"I…I was about to leave…for yoga…" she said and rubbed her neck under the ponytail nervously.

"It won't take long."

I walked past her inside, and she closed the door, still slightly worried. "What is this about?"

"Can we sit?" I asked and pointed at her dining room table. She nodded, still fiddling with the small hairs on her neck.

"Sure. Do you want anything? Coffee?"

I smiled politely. "I don't think we have time for that if you don't want to miss your yoga class."

She shrugged. "I can make some real quick."

"Then I won't say no to that."

Kristin disappeared into the kitchen and came back with two cups of coffee. She placed a cup in front of me, spilling a little on the table as she did, then wiping it away with a paper towel and a nervous chuckle.

I sipped my cup. "Wonderful coffee."

She sat down in the chair next to mine while I opened the case file and showed her a picture of Kate Taylor taken ten years ago, just a few months before she disappeared.

"I believe you know her?"

She swallowed when seeing her friend. "K-Kate? Is that what this is about? But it was so long ago."

"I know, but the case was never closed," I said. "I take it you've heard about her son, Nick?"

Kristin nodded, warming her hands on the sides of the cup, even though it wasn't very cold in her house.

"Yes. Awful tragedy. I can't believe it."

"Well, it has me wondering too, and that's why I am here. I was hoping you could shed some light on the family. What would make Nick bring a gun to church and try to shoot his father?"

Chapter 21

"I...I don't really know much about them," she started, fiddling with her cup. "I mean, it's been so many years now, and I hardly knew much even back then. I'm not sure I can be of much help, to be honest."

I nodded. "I understand. I was just...well, worried that there was something we were missing here."

She sipped her cup. "Like what, Detective?"

I exhaled and folded my hands on top of the file. "I don't know. That maybe Nick tried to hurt his father for the simple reason that he knew he had killed his mother?"

Kristin stared at me, her eyes growing big. She shook her head. "Detective, I don't really think...why would you say that? He was cleared back then. He had an alibi."

I looked at the papers in the file. "He was at a conference, yes. In Atlanta."

She nodded and smiled. "Yes, that was it. He was very far away. I don't really see how he could have..."

"But what if he did?" I asked, deliberately provocative. "What if he somehow managed to kill her anyway? How was their relationship? You said in your statement that she needed to *blow off some steam*. Both you and your friend, Joan, used that same expression, oddly enough. But what does that even mean?"

Kristin stared up at me, her eyes searching mine, her tongue playing with the inside of her cheek.

"I guess it meant she wasn't doing very well in her marriage."

"Why not? Were they fighting a lot?"

"I…I guess. Or maybe she just found him to be extremely boring," she said.

"And she wanted out? You said she wanted to disappear, right?"

She nodded, sipping more coffee, her lips quivering slightly. "Y-yes. I think she killed herself. I think she got drunk that night then drowned herself."

I stared at her. Now, it was my turn to scrutinize her. "But why, Kristin? Why would your friend kill herself? Why not just get a divorce?"

"I…I don't know."

"I'll tell you. I'll tell you what I think. I think she was scared of him. No, more than that, she was terrified of her own husband, and she told you this on the trip. She didn't dare to leave him. And you're terrified of him too, aren't you? That's why you haven't told anyone that you, too, believe he killed her. Because he has been threatening you, am I right?"

She shook her head. "I…I don't really…"

"It's okay. You don't have to. It's not your job to figure these things out. It's mine. But if he really killed his wife, then I'm taking him down for it, one way or another, with or without your help."

I paused and sipped my coffee, not allowing myself to

get too agitated. There was nothing worse in my book than a man abusing his wife. And this guy would even let his son go down before he told the truth.

I looked into the case file, then pulled out a piece of paper I had printed before getting here and showed it to her.

"Do you know anything about this?"

She looked at it, then shook her head. "What is this?"

"I found this in Nick's files. Apparently, the DCF had their eyes on the family. Back when Nick was four years old, his school reported that the boy was engaging in troublesome behavior. He had asked a girl to strip down naked for him in the bathroom, then told her to lick the toilet seat. The DCF investigated the family and found odd bruises on the child, and he told them stories of him being forced to punish himself when he was bad and cut his skin with razor blades, then being forced to spend an entire night in a small bathroom, only allowed to drink from the toilet bowl. The DCF supervised the family for months but found nothing and concluded it was just stories that the boy had made up. The parents had explanations for all the bruises since the boy got them riding his bike or climbing trees, and the cuts were some he had inflicted on himself, they said before they stopped him. DCF ended up believing them and left the family alone. Now, my question to you is this: Did you know, Kristin? Did you know this was happening in their home?"

Kristin was no longer looking at me. She was shaking her head and crying. "I knew the DCF had been on their case. Kate told me about it; she said the boy had told a bunch of lies and that it would all blow over eventually. Andrew was angry about it, and I sensed Kate was scared too, scared of losing the boy, but she just didn't want to admit it. I don't know. I just assumed she was right, that it was nothing but a bunch of lies that the boy had come up with."

"But deep down inside, you knew something was off in that family, didn't you? When you visited them, the way Kate never wanted to talk about them, how she seemed troubled at times. Did she have bruises too? Did she?"

Kristin swallowed, her head still bent. Then she nodded. "She had these cuts on her arm that looked like they were made by razor blades. I didn't know what to think. She didn't want to talk about them, so we just didn't. There was also the time she had bruises on her upper arms like someone had grabbed her, hard. There were other things too, cuts in strange places, like right on her bikini line when we went to the beach. She had excuses for all of them."

"And you pretended to believe her because it was easier that way, am I right?" I asked.

Kristin sniffled and nodded. "Yes. You're right. I'm not proud of it, but it's the truth. In the end, we barely noticed anymore. But it definitely got worse and worse."

"Do you still see each other? You and Joan? Are you still friends?" I asked.

She shook her head. "We haven't seen one another since...that trip. I heard she was divorced, moved, and got married to some other guy."

"That explains why it's been hard to track her down. So, you don't know where I can find her?"

She shook her head again, grabbed a tissue from a box, and blew her nose. "I'm afraid not."

I got up and looked at my watch. "All right. Thank you so much, Kristin. You've been a great help."

"You really think he killed her, do you?" she asked once

again as I walked toward the door. "Even though he had an alibi?"

I nodded, halfway out the door, then paused. "I do. Somehow, he managed to get away with the perfect murder."

Chapter 22

I walked into Fowler's office, forgetting to knock. I had just gotten back from my meeting with Kristin Grant and bought a sandwich on my way back that I still hadn't eaten. I was holding it in my hand as I walked inside.

Fowler looked up at me, then pointed toward the two empty chairs.

"Sit."

I did. Fowler looked at me from across the mahogany table. He pressed the tips of his fingers against each other.

"I don't quite know how to tell you this."

"I'm a big boy," I said. "I can take it. Is it about last night? Any news about the guy who broke into my house? Have the hospitals called back? Have they found a guy who was shot in the thigh?"

"Easy there, cowboy," Fowler said, shaking his head. "I have had no luck finding him yet, no. But that doesn't mean we won't. He'll turn up sooner or later. I have a word out to all the stations, and they'll let me know the

83

names of anyone who didn't show up for work today. We'll get him. One way or another."

I exhaled, annoyed. I had hoped for good news. I had no idea what to tell my family if I went back home and he hadn't been found. Josie was terrified that he was going to come back. And to be frank, so was I.

"So, what is this about? Why have you called me in?"

"It's about the boy."

"Nick?"

"Yes, him. His dad was here earlier. We had told him to bring in Nick's computer and his phone, so we could go through it all to find out if he had planned to bring the gun to hurt more people, or if he was fascinated by mass shooters and maybe frequented any of the websites where they chat and cheer each other on, you know stuff like that. Well, we didn't find any of that, but his dad presented us with some pretty damaging material. He said he knew we'd find it anyway, so he might as well show it to us. He had already gone through his son's social media accounts by himself in anger because he wanted to know what Nick was up to, and that's when he found all this stuff. He said he thought about deleting it because he wanted to protect Nick, but then decided against it since he believed the boy needed to take the punishment for his actions. It's about time he learns that his actions have consequences, he said."

"Really?" I said suspiciously.

"Yes, really. I know you believe your boy here is innocent…"

"I'm not saying he's innocent," I interrupted him. "I'm just saying that he shot his dad because he thought there was no other way. And I'm trying to find out why he felt that way. And, actually, I've been getting closer…"

"I'm gonna stop you right there," he said, "because what we have here is a gamechanger."

I wrinkled my forehead. "What do you mean?"

Fowler lifted a hand to stop me. He grabbed the phone and dialed a number, then spoke into it.

"Do you have it ready? Can you send me the files?"

There was an answer, and Fowler hung up. "I've had the IT guys working on it for the past few hours, and they have the files ready for us now. You might want to eat that sandwich first because after this, you'll have lost your appetite."

Chapter 23

A REDHAIRED GIRL looked into the camera on her phone. She was crying, her narrow, bloodshot eyes looking at us while she was pleading.

"Please," she said. "Please, don't make me do this."

Then she leaned over, placed her tongue on the toilet seat, and started licking, still while crying. Once done, she put her head inside the bowl and flushed while her head was still in it.

Crying, she lifted her head, then cried out: "I'm a worthless whore; please, take care of me, Daddy."

Clip to the next video. Another girl. This one was blonde. She, too, was crying while filming herself. She filmed herself naked on the floor of the bathroom as she peed into a plastic cup.

Then, she drank it.

The next video showed a girl cutting herself on the arm with a razor blade while crying. The letters she cut were shaping the word:

Whore.

In the last video, we watched a girl as she took a toilet brush. Then—crying heavily—she put it in her mouth.

"Okay, okay," I said and turned away from Fowler's computer screen, suddenly pleased I had listened to him and eaten my sandwich before we watched the videos. "I've seen enough. What in the world is that?"

"They call it *hurtcore*," he said. "Girls, who, against their will, are pressured into humiliating themselves while filming it."

"And you got these videos from Nick's computer?"

Fowler nodded. "And his phone. You can see the texts he sent to the girls as well. I made a transcript of one. Look here. You see how he tells her to kneel by the toilet and flush while her head is still inside of it. Then he tells her what to say, to call herself a worthless whore, and she's pleading with him to stop it. His only answer is that her pleading turns him on. He asks her to film herself while she's crying, then hit herself and strangle herself and tell herself that she's *just a stupid whore*. In one of them, he even asks her to put the toilet brush up inside of her and eat her own feces, but I thought that was a little too much for you to watch."

"And they do it?" I asked.

Needless to say, I was disgusted—on the verge of throwing up.

He nodded. "Yes. Because they have no choice, or they don't think they have. He meets them through Skype or messenger or on Instagram or TikTok, wherever he can find them, and they start out as friends. He tells them he likes them and grooms them slowly until they're ready. Then, he sweet-talks them into sending him nude photos of themselves or even videos. They do it because they have low self-esteem, and because they think he likes them. Then, as soon as he has the video or the photos, he starts pressuring them. He tells them he'll send the video or the pictures to her family and her friends. He threatens to post it on social media, so everyone will see, and that's when the humiliation begins. They plead with him not to, and then he can persuade them to do anything he'd like to see—humiliating themselves. These are broken girls, Hunter. You've got to be really broken down to do something like this. And some of these girls are minors. They're not much older than Josie, for crying out loud. It's sick! This guy is a pervert, Hunter. He's nothing but a predator, and I'll see to it that he is put away for a very, *very* long time. Mark my words. You are done trying to save him; do you hear me? Done."

Chapter 24

I HAD no idea what to believe. As soon as I was done at Fowler's office, I ran to the parking lot where I had parked my bike, then got on it and roared into the street. I drove it through town, zigzagging my way through traffic, going through what Fowler had told me in my head.

Could it really be true? Could the boy I had seen really have done those awful things to those girls?

It didn't seem possible.

Yet, the evidence was there. Right on Fowler's computer. Video after video extracted from the boy's computer and phone. Text after text where he degraded them to nothing but objects, dolls he could treat however he wanted.

Fowler was right; it was sick, and there was no way I could explain my way out of this. There were no more excuses.

I parked in front of the detention center and walked up to the back door. The woman behind the glass saw my badge, then called for someone to lead me down the hallway and back into the room with the barren walls and tables that were bolted to the floor.

I waited for about ten minutes until the door opened. Nick had a big bruise on his cheek as he approached me and sat down, his eyes looking at the floor, not at me.

I stared down at him, my nostrils flaring, the images still flickering for my inner eye, images and videos I would never escape.

"Look at me, Nick," I said, trying to keep calm. "Look at me."

The boy lifted his eyes.

"You remember me, right? You said so the last time I was here. I tried to help you in church, and I have even tried to help you out there, trying to figure out why on earth a young boy like you would shoot your own dad. And now they tell me you've been hurting young women online? What do you have to say for yourself, Nick!"

The boy looked at me, then shook his head. "I don't know what you're talking about.

I slammed my fist onto the metal table. "Yes, you do! Don't lie to me."

He crumpled down in fear, shaking his head. "No. I don't. What videos?"

"The ones they found on your computer of the girls humiliating themselves, doing only what you told them to do, what you blackmailed them to do, breaking their poor spirits."

"I…I don't understand," he said.

"They found them on your computer and your phone. Don't give me that innocent act. Was it because that's what your dad did to you? Because you went through the same thing in your childhood? And now you're just repeating it? In some sick vicious circle? Like people becoming molesters because their parents were? Did your dad do those things to you, Nick?"

Nick exhaled. His eyes were filling.

"Did your dad tell you to lick the toilet seat? Did he lock you in the bathroom, and have you drink out of the bowl? Did he tell you to cut yourself with razor blades? Did he, Nick? Nick? Darn it, Nick, talk to me."

Nick shook his head. "I…I don't know. I don't remember…"

"But the DCF suspected it. In your file, they said you told them those things. When you were four years old, you said these things were done to you. Were they right? Was it your father? Was that why you pulled that gun on him? Did he torture you and your mother and then kill her, did he? Nick?"

"YES!" he yelled, then bent forward like he was in pain, talking through a curtain of tears. "Yes, he did all of those things! I knew no one would ever believe me like they didn't believe me back then. That's why I shot him. There was no other way for him to be punished for what he had done."

"How did you know, Nick? How did you find out he killed your mother?" I asked, my heart pounding in my chest. Finally, I was getting somewhere in this case. It wasn't pleasant what was being revealed, but it had to see the light of day. "How did you realize it?"

Nick leaned forward like he was telling me a secret, and no one else could hear. But it was just us there, and the guard, who didn't seem to care even a little bit.

"I've always known but never dared to say anything. I suggest you ask his new wife."

Chapter 25

"ARE YOU DETECTIVE HUNTER?"

I had just walked out the front door of the building housing our police department on my way to my bike. It was late in the afternoon now, and I was running late for Camille's treatment. I almost rushed past him without seeing him. But as he addressed me, I recognized him right away. When someone gets shot in front of you, you tend to remember their face forever. Same goes when they're the main suspect of your investigation.

"Mr. Taylor? What are you doing here?"

He was smaller than I remembered him yet seemed bigger because of how well trained he was underneath his suit. He had a sharp jawline like his son and big bushy eyebrows that I suspected Nick would get one day too.

He exhaled. His flaring nostrils, along with the vein in his forehead, told me he was agitated. I stayed a few steps away from him. He pointed a finger at me. I didn't move. His gesture was aggressive, and I didn't want him to think I was scared of him. I was twice his size.

He spoke through gritted teeth.

"It has got to stop."

"Excuse me? What has got to stop?"

He growled angrily. "This. You. Whatever it is you're doing."

"I don't know. What am I doing?"

I looked at my watch. I was so late for my appointment with Camille and had put my hope in traffic being light enough for me to make it anyway. Now, we were going to be late if I didn't break a few traffic regulations on my way home.

"My son is sick, Detective. Don't believe anything he says."

I wrinkled my forehead. "What do you mean he's sick?"

"He's a pathological liar, Detective. He does this. He's been doing it all his life. Ever since he was a kid, he'd lie to his teachers and tell them these stories."

"So, you're telling me he's lying when he tells me he was abused as a child?" I asked bluntly, then waited for his reaction.

It came pretty fast. His eyes went blank for a second, then fired up in rage. I could tell he was trying to keep himself composed, but failing miserably. Everything inside of him exploded while he bit down, trying to stifle it by clenching his fists. He lifted one up toward me, but it barely reached my face.

"I...How dare you!"

"How dare you...sir? Torturing a little child? Murdering your wife?"

Andrew Taylor stared at me. The fist came down, and he pulled back. It was obvious he was taken aback by my words. That was the point. I wanted him to know that I knew what kind of a person he was and that I was going to expose him.

"Is that what he told you? And you…you believe him? How? Why? The boy is not well. You must know this. Didn't you see the videos from his computer and phone? Didn't you see what kind of a sick monster he is? How he abused those girls and humiliated them? That is the kind of person he is. You saw it with your own eyes. He tried to kill me, Detective. I'm the victim here. He's sick, just like his mom was too. My son belongs behind bars. I hate to admit it, but that is where he should stay, and I suggest you keep it that way. Don't you understand? He never liked the fact that I remarried. He hates my wife, and now he's trying to get back at me this way, trying first to shoot me, then tell anyone stupid enough to listen that his dad is an abuser and a murderer. Don't tell me you're actually buying into it? Are you that stupid, Detective?"

I looked down at the man in front of me in the blue suit and yellow tie. Yes, I wanted to slap him across the face; I wanted to hurt him. For what I believed he had done to his son while growing up, and how he had abused and probably murdered his wife. But this was not the time or place. Justice would come soon enough. And that's when he'd be taken down.

I lifted my arm and looked at my watch. "I have somewhere to be. If you'll excuse me, I don't have time for this."

Andrew Taylor scoffed as I pushed my way past him, hitting my upper arm against his shoulder, pushing him aside.

"You're a fool for believing him, Detective; don't you see? He's using you!" he yelled after me, but I was no longer listening. I got on my bike, then roared it to life and put my helmet on, ignoring him. As I rode it across the parking lot, I could still hear him yelling, his voice growing smaller and smaller behind me.

Chapter 26

WE WERE FIFTEEN MINUTES LATE, and Dr. Kendrick wasn't very pleased with us as we rushed inside, me pushing Camille in the wheelchair even though she didn't need it that much anymore and walked mostly on her own. She still couldn't run, at least not yet.

"I am so sorry," I said as she gave me that look, arms crossed. "Something came up at work."

"You have been late to every afternoon treatment for the past week now," she said. "That means other patients' treatments who are scheduled after her will be pushed too."

"I know. I am sorry."

Dr. Kendrick sent me a compassionate smile. "I know it's not easy to have to come in twice a day."

"I wish we could just do all of it at once," I said while the assistants helped Camille get in the chamber and closed the lid with a low shush. Camille's eyes locked with mine as it closed. I knew she didn't enjoy the claustrophobic feeling right after it was locked, knowing she couldn't get out, but after a few minutes, she would usually calm down and be able to relax.

"Why can't we just do an entire week of treatments at once?"

Dr. Kendrick nodded. "I get that a lot. But we can't leave her in there for too long. Wouldn't be good."

"What would happen?"

Dr. Kendrick pushed a button on the instruments, and the air hissed in the steel cylinder. "Well, we have to do this with oxygen at high atmospheric pressure, so at first, it would damage her ears...possibly burst her eardrums, and we won't want that to happen. It could also change her vision or collapse her lungs. Oxygen toxicity or poisoning could occur; too much oxygen in the body's tissues can cause convulsions and other complications. It can damage the central nervous system, and in severe cases, cause death. So, that's why we're very cautious. But I am so happy to see the big progress in your wife. It's truly remarkable. We'd like to write her story for a medical paper after we're done here. Would she be willing to participate in that?"

I smiled and glanced at my wife inside the chamber. Her eyes were closed now, and I knew she was resting.

"Why don't you ask her yourself?" I said. "She is capable of answering for herself now."

It was true. She had been speaking more and more over the past week or so, and she was able to use entire sentences now. It was like she was finally truly coming back to us...like she was slowly becoming herself again.

Dr. Kendrick smiled and nodded. "Very well. We'll do that when we get closer then. Her story is truly remarkable, and we're trying to get this treatment FDA approved for brain injury, so I am hoping her story can help that process and maybe speed it along so other patients can get it too and maybe even get their insurance to pay for it. So many come here knowing this is a chance for help, but they can't afford it, and they leave emptyhanded. I hate to see that, knowing I can actually help them. It's heartbreaking."

"I can understand how it must be," I said, then sat down in my usual chair, pulling up my computer and placed it in my lap. Camille's treatments had become a time for me to really dig into my work, and I was beginning to enjoy those little moments of quietness in my life. I still thought about the meeting with Nick's father earlier and shivered when thinking about what the boy had told me at the detention center. I opened the case files and looked through them again, then reached into my briefcase and pulled out the old file on the murder case of Kate Taylor. I had asked to have her autopsy sent over from the ME's office in Key West and needed to go through it. As I read through it, one line, in particular, grabbed my attention and wouldn't let go. I kept reading it over and over again, then stared at Camille inside her chamber before returning to it. I flipped a page, then looked at the next one, searching for another detail, then found it. I stared at the words on the page, wondering if I had just discovered the proof that she was, in fact, murdered, and how it was done.

The problem was that it made absolutely no sense to me.

Chapter 27

"AND THEN YOU look up at me with those big brown eyes of yours, and you say to me, *you do realize you have it in your hand, don't you?*"

Camille burst into laughter, and Josie joined in, laughing wholeheartedly. It was becoming an everyday thing for Josie to ask her mother to tell her stories from back when she was just a young child during dinner. And I had a feeling it was one of Camille's favorite moments of the day as well. To me, it was more than that. It was everything. Watching them reconnect was my favorite thing in the whole world.

"I can't believe you did that, Mommy," Josie said and ate her noodles. We had brought home Chinese food today. We had been eating a lot of take-out food lately since it was impossible for me to make it to Camille's treatments and cook dinner as well, so even though it meant we ate a lot of the same food, it was what was possible these days. And it worked fine. Gave us plenty of time to talk till Camille got tired and needed to get back into her bed.

"It's true," I said. "I was there. I'm a witness."

Josie gave me an endearing look. She had been so happy lately, and it was a joy to see. Being fourteen wasn't an easy age, to put it mildly. But ever since her mother got better, there had been less of those meltdowns, and the rolling of eyes and growling had subsided for a little while too. I knew it would be back eventually, of course, it would. Teenagers would be teenagers, and I just enjoyed the way things were right now until it changed back.

I rose to my feet and grabbed the plates, then walked to the kitchen to wash them off and put them in the dishwasher, while Josie asked her mother for another story.

"Don't forget your homework," I said to her. "Your mom needs to rest soon too, baby."

"Please, Dad?" she asked. "Just one more story. I only have math and science. It's so easy."

I chuckled. I didn't know of any other teenage girls who'd call math and science easy. And she was even in advanced classes in both subjects, yet it still seemed like it was almost too easy for her.

"All right," I said and closed the dishwasher. "Just one more story then."

"Yay. With pictures. I want to look at pictures too," she said, then rushed to the shelves in the living room and pulled down a photo album. She hurried back to her mother and opened it, then flipped a couple of pages till she found one she liked and pointed at it.

"This one. What are we doing here? How old am I?"

Camille glanced at the picture, then smiled warmly. As it turned out, remembering things from her past was very good for Camille's rehabilitation as well.

"That one," Camille said. "Is from our trip to Key West. You were…four, I think? Right, Harry?"

I nodded and wiped my hands on a dishtowel, then walked back to look at it over her shoulder. A very young

Josie stared back at me from a white sandy beach, wearing goggles, a determined look on her face.

"You loved watching the fishies in the water down there," I said. "You could spend hours watching them."

"And your dad was fishing," Camille said. "But you didn't like that he would catch the fish, and you would always tell him to throw them back."

"I wanted to eat them, but you would hear nothing of it," I said with a light chuckle.

Camille flipped a page. "Look, there you are, holding a baby hammerhead shark. You caught that with your bare hands in the water."

"I think I remember this," Josie said. "I threw it back out in the water, didn't I?"

"You sure did," I said and looked at my beautiful daughter. This was one of those moments you just wanted to last forever. I was so happy in this very second that I paid very little attention to the screeching tires in the street outside.

Chapter 28

THE MICROWAVE BEEPED, and Jean got up. She pulled out her dish. It was supposed to be some kind of chicken and mashed potatoes, but she couldn't really tell which was the chicken and which were the potatoes, and the gravy seemed more greenish than brown. She stared down at the plastic tray and its contents, then decided to toss it in the trash. She made herself a sandwich instead, while glaring at the house next door, wondering what they were doing in there. She wondered what they were having for dinner and whether Josie needed help with her Spanish homework.

Let it go, Jean.

Spread out on the table behind her were listings for rentals in Savannah, Georgia. Jean had a sister living up there and thought it was time she moved closer to her. She had seen a couple of job listings searching for a nurse up in the area as well and applied for some of them. They weren't as exciting as the one she had working the ER in Miami, and they paid less too, but it was what she needed right now. She had to move on.

It was time.

Jean sat down and ate the sandwich while reading through the rental listings. There was a nice little town-house in walking distance from the center of Savannah, close to restaurants. It had a nice porch outside and was built in that old Victorian style she loved so much.

Jean smiled and took another bite of her sandwich. She imagined herself living there, sitting out on the porch on the swing, or walking to downtown and going out to dinner or even just for a cup of coffee.

Jean had always been drawn to Savannah and knew that if she didn't live in Miami, that's where she'd go. Often when visiting her sister, who lived about half an hour outside of the town, she had taken trips to Savannah and loved just walking the streets there, looking at the pretty old houses with their wrought-iron porches and Spanish moss hanging from the trees. It would be a new start for her, a brand-new life, and it was exactly what she needed.

Get away from the old.

Jean walked to the window and looked out at her old street. She had lived there for almost twenty years now. She still liked it there; she had to admit. Yet she had that sense inside of her that she was done with it; she was done with Miami.

And with Harry Hunter.

Yes, she was going to miss him and Josie. It was going to be hard for the first couple of months, but it was better than staying here and having her heart broken every time she saw either one of them.

Anything would be better than here.

Jean finished her sandwich while looking into the street, thinking about the first time she and Harry had met when he and Camille had just moved in. Jean had not been very excited to get new neighbors since she enjoyed her privacy and being in her yard without anyone seeing her. The house had been empty for years, and she liked it that way. She avoided them for the first couple of days after she saw the truck arrive, thinking the last thing she wanted was to get tricked into having to help them carry their stuff.

But then one day, a young woman, pregnant on the verge of bursting, had knocked on her door, asking if she had a couple of eggs because she was baking. As soon as Jean had opened the door and looked into the woman's eyes, she knew she couldn't resent her. As Harry came over later to give her the eggs back, she realized she was going to love those two forever. But mostly him. As Jean stood there thinking about it, she realized she had loved him from the second she stood face to face with him on that porch. She hadn't wanted to admit it back then because he was married, and she really liked Camille, especially after they began to hang out almost every day, drinking coffee or later having a glass of wine. Jean had kept it to herself that her heart beat just a little faster when he was nearby, or how she'd jump in happiness when hearing his voice.

You need to get out of here, fast, girl, she thought to herself as she looked into the street, a tear caught in the corner of her eye that she didn't allow to escape. She grabbed her phone and checked her emails, seeing if there were any responses from the jobs she had applied for or the rentals she had written to. She sighed and thought about her new life instead, trying hard to get excited about it, when she heard the tires screeching. She lifted her eyes and saw the car drive into the road, then rush past Harry's house, opening fire.

Chapter 29

RA-TA-DA-DA. Ra-ta-da. Ra-ta-da. Ra-ta-da-da!

The sound was deafening, and it felt like it went on for hours, even though it was probably just for a few seconds—a few crucial and potentially fatal seconds.

Ra-ta-da-da. Ra-ta-da. Ra-ta-da. Ra-ta-da-da!

It kept going, on and on, for an eternity.

I had realized it too late. I had ignored the sound of the tires on the asphalt outside, thinking it was just some idiot burning rubber, showing off for his friends or some girlfriend he was trying to impress.

It had never occurred to me that this could happen. Not to me, not here, not in this nice neighborhood. But now it did, and as I realized what was really going on, I threw myself at Josie, pushing her to the floor, letting my big massive body cover her, while the sound of the bullets splintering the wood outside, tearing holes in the door and shattering the windows, drowned out her screams from beneath me.

Ra-ta-da-da. Ra-ta-da. Ra-ta-da. Ra-ta-da-da!

I screamed at the top of my lungs, and so did Josie and

Camille. Camille had fallen to the floor and lay flat, face-down on the wooden planks next to us. But she was in the open, not covered by furniture the way we were. She was exposed but paralyzed by fear, unable to move. She stared at me, scared out of her wits, then reached out her hand toward us and grabbed Josie's in hers.

And then she screamed.

A bullet ripped through the tip of her shoulder, tearing the flesh open with a loud, almost whistling sound.

"MOM!" Josie screamed when seeing this. "MOOOM! NOOO!"

Meanwhile, the sound continued outside. Endlessly.

Ra-ta-da-da. Ra-ta-da. Ra-ta-da. Ra-ta-da-da!

Another bullet whispered through the air and hit Camille on the floor. Seeing the blood, and how her body spasmed, I screamed.

"NO! Camille! No!"

Camille withered in pain. Blood was gushing from her wounds, soaking the wooden floor beneath her.

I yelled through the rain of bullets while crawling toward her, making sure Josie was covered behind the couch.

"I am not losing you once again!"

I wormed my way across the floor, reached out my hand to grab Camille's, and pulled her, sliding her body across the wooden floor, when a bullet smashed through the window closest to us, whistled through the air and grazed her neck, then continued and ended in the wall behind us.

Crying, I pulled Camille behind the couch, next to Josie, but then realized my shirt was soaked. I gasped and stared at her neck, where blood was gushing.

"Oh, dear Lord, no!"

As the sound of gunfire subsided as quickly as it had

started, I pressed my hand against the wound, trying to stop the bleeding, while screaming at Josie.

"CALL 9-1-1!"

In the second I had yelled the words, the back door burst open, and someone stormed inside. A heartbeat went by, and I held my breath.

Jean's shrill voice cut through the air.

"Harry? Josie?"

A sigh of relief went through me, then fear set in—the fear of losing Camille all over again.

"In here. We need help. Please, help us!"

Chapter 30

I FELT like we had become regulars at the Jackson Memorial Hospital the past few years. I, for one, had spent enough time in there, waiting for news of my loved ones, paralyzed with fear, with no other tools to help me but my prayers.

I was bent over, mumbling under my breath, pleading with God not to take Camille away again when I felt Jean's hand on my shoulder.

"I'm sure she'll be okay."

I lifted my head and looked at Jean, then at her bloody clothes. The front of her white T-shirt was completely soaked, and Camille's blood was smeared on her arms and face. She even had some in her hair. Jean had managed to stop the bleeding using a dishtowel and applying constant pressure to the wound before the ambulance came. The paramedics had told me they believed that might have saved Camille from bleeding out and maybe even saved her life.

Again, she came to our rescue. How could I ever thank her enough?

"It was scary," she said.

Jean's frightened eyes lingered on me.

"When will this ever end, Harry?"

I shook my head in disbelief. "When I shut up."

She leaned back with a deep exhale. "I can't believe they'd…I mean…come on!"

I nodded in agreement. It was, by far, one of the scariest minutes of my life. Luckily, both Josie and I had made it through without a scratch. She was sitting in a chair on the other side of me, eyes staring blankly into the air, in a state of complete shock. I put my arm around her and pulled her close. Her body was shaking in my arms, but she wasn't crying. She was just staring into thin air, barely even blinking, hardly breathing.

"Maybe it's time I cave in," I said, addressed to Jean. "Maybe I've reached my limit now."

She sat up straight and gave me one of her looks, reminding me of my mother the time I had told her I was going to quit playing baseball because someone on the team was picking on me. I had trouble running fast because I had grown so much very fast and become clumsy and unable to control my long limbs almost overnight.

"You listen to me," she had said back then, giving me that exact same look. "If you give in to a bully, you empower him. You give him complete power over you. Instead, you show them what you're made of, Harry. You become the best and the fastest."

And so, I did. Once I realized those long legs could be used for running really fast, I had become the star of the team within months, and no one bullied me again. I still knew this to be true; you shouldn't give in just because you go through resistance or because people were pushing against you. But this was different. This was becoming dangerous.

"Don't you dare even say that," Jean said. "I will not hear those words leave your lips again, Harry Hunter."

It was always serious with Jean when she called me by my full name. That's when she meant business…when she wanted to be sure I was listening.

"I have to think about my family, about Josie," I said and glanced down at her in my arms. "I don't think I can justify this any longer."

"You listen to me, Harry Hunter," she said. "These people almost killed you and your entire family tonight. You don't let them get away with this, you hear me? This is not you. This is the fear talking. Don't let fear do the talking for you. Fear is a coward. Faith is the warrior, and you're a warrior, Harry. Have faith. And then do your part. Bring them down, all of them this time."

"But how?" I asked, throwing out my hands. "How am I supposed to do that? I'm talking to the FBI. I'm helping them all I can, but even they keep running into walls of silence. No one dares to rat on their colleagues. They've tried to follow the money trail and so far, arrested a couple of officers from our district, but they've only just scratched the surface. I have a feeling this goes way deeper. If only there were something else I could do…"

She nodded, then pulled out her phone from her pocket. "Maybe this can help."

She found a video and played it for me. "I was on my phone right when it happened, checking emails. I saw the car, driving fast down our street, tires screeching loudly. I don't know why, but something compelled me to do it. I turned on the camera and started recording right before they began shooting. Look."

She turned the video on, and I watched as the blue car rushed down the street, then slowed down right in front of my house, and some type of automatic rifle was pushed out through the window, then began to shoot. It all went by so fast; it seemed impossible that it was the same incident that I had experienced inside my house. Being in there, fearing for my family's and my life had felt like an eternity…like it would never stop. In the video, it took less than a minute.

But the picture was very clear of the car, and as I looked in through the window, my heart began to beat so fast I feared it might explode.

Chapter 31

I DECIDED to stay the night at the hospital, while Jean took Josie home. Jean drove Josie to my dad's place, where she'd spend the night while a forensics team took care of our house. Josie needed her sleep, and there was no reason for her to stay. The doctor had told us Camille was going to be okay. She had lost a lot of blood, and they had to stitch her up on her shoulder and neck, but she was going to be fine. They were all superficial wounds, and there was no severe damage done or any fractures. She had been very lucky, he said. Also, to have an ER nurse as a neighbor to stop the bleeding in time.

"It was all just a very happy ending," he said.

I didn't know about happy or ending since I had a feeling this was far from over yet.

I waited until Camille was out of surgery around three a.m., then went with her into the room they gave her and waited for her to wake up from the anesthesia. Around four a.m., she was fully awake, her brown eyes looking at me. I couldn't – for the life of me—understand how she could look so beautiful even with what she had been through. But she did. She was gorgeous, as always. She parted her lips like she wanted to speak.

I shushed her while pulling up the covers.

"You need to rest, Camille. We'll talk later."

She put her hand on my arm, then squeezed it to stop me.

"No."

I paused. "What do you mean, no? You're beginning to sound like your teenage daughter; do you know that?"

She looked at me, her eyes strained, painful.

"I…need to tell you the truth. About me. I owe this to you. You've been nothing but good to me."

I shook my head. "Nonsense. You don't owe me anything. I don't need to know. At least not now. We can talk about it later."

I looked away, biting my cheek. I realized my hands were shaking. I had wanted answers, but now that she was offering them to me, I wasn't sure I wanted them anymore. I was terrified of what they might do to me, how I might react. I wasn't even sure I wanted to know anymore.

Because I feared it would destroy everything. Destroy me and my family.

"But I need to," she said. "I need to tell you the truth, no matter what it might do to me, what it might do to us."

I shook my head. She sent me a weak smile.

"It's time, Harry. No more lies. No more secrets. These people almost killed me a second time tonight, trying to shut me up, wanting to shut both of us up. But it was mostly me because I have the knowledge to take them down. I am dangerous to them, and we both know this."

I stared at her, my nostrils flaring, not knowing what to do. I grabbed a chair from the corner of the room and sat down next to her bed, holding her delicate hand tightly in mine, pressing back my fears, bracing myself for what was about to hit me.

"All right. I guess we're doing this, then."

Chapter 32

"GROWING up in the Dominican Republic, all people ever dreamed about was coming to America. Where I grew up, sexual abuse was like second-hand smoke. It was everywhere. You couldn't escape it. You knew one day it would catch up to you. I was exploited by a couple of my father's friends, and he let them do it, even received money from them. He was a pimp, not just for me, but for numerous other girls in our neighborhood. It was normal. My granddad was a pimp, and when my brother turned thirteen, he was told he was going to be a pimp too. It was just the way things were where we lived. I knew that I had only two choices. Either I became a prostitute, or I became a pimp. There were no other possibilities, no other way. I remember seeing the people involved in trafficking in their new cars, their big houses, throwing money around downtown. They were living the life. So, I decided I didn't want to live my life as a victim anymore. When I turned eighteen, I decided I was done being exploited, and I wanted to make a life for myself. And I was good at it. I would approach girls in the street or at the mall, and they'd let me because I was a woman, a beautiful woman. I was nice, and why would some nice woman not be someone you could trust? I would pick the prettiest girl, sitting by herself. I'd tell her she had beautiful eyes. If she said thank you, I'd leave. But if she told me, 'No, I don't,' I knew I had her. I looked for the broken ones, the ones easy to persuade, the ones who would want a new life for themselves. So, I told them I could get them a modeling job and told them to come with me to the harbor, where my brother waited with the rest of his team. They'd stack them in boats and transport them to the U.S. coast. I would get my share of the money, and I began saving up. I wanted to get away. I wanted to travel to the U.S. I wanted to go to university, a real American university, FIT. I wanted to become an engineer. And this was my way. It was the only way. There was a lot of money to be made this way. And it wasn't just young girls. We helped families fulfill their dreams of going to America, of starting over. We helped them get there, and that made me feel good about myself. They were achieving what I could only dream of. Every time I watched that boat leave at night, I would dream of it one day being me onboard, fulfilling my destiny. The power of the dream was so strong, it became a longing, a yearning, and I would often lie awake at night fantasizing about it, wanting it so bad I could scream. One day, when I had enough money, I told my brother to put me on board his boat. I handed him all my savings and told him I wanted to go. He looked at me, then shook his head. You know what he said? He said, "Can't do it. You're the best one we've got." He wouldn't let me go because he didn't want to lose me and what I could do. It would be bad for his business. So, you know what I did? I went to his competitor, another guy whom I knew smuggled out refugees, and paid him instead. He took me on his boat along with maybe a hundred other refugees, with nothing but the clothes we wore and the dream in our minds. He took me to the coast of America, and then they threw us overboard, telling us to swim the rest of the way. So, we did. Not many made it. I did. I remember sitting on the beach north of here, holding the white sand between my fingers, thinking I made it, I finally made it. I also remember a body that had washed up close to me, then realized it wouldn't be long before they'd come for us. So, I ran. I ran and hid and became a homeless person in Miami. Living in abandoned buildings, I met many people. One of them told me he could help me make money. And it wasn't prostitution. He took me to the harbor, where I met with Ferdinand, the guy from your work, and that other man, Wolfe, was there too. Ferdinand said he had work for me if I wanted it. They wanted me to go back and forth between the U.S. and Santo Domingo in the Dominican Republic, and help with the transport. I had an advantage because I was local, and they needed someone they could trust to handle the other side. I didn't have to stay there, just go once or twice a month. If I did this, he would be able to give me a social security number and a passport. I would become an American. I didn't even think about it for one second. I had to get off the streets. I had to make a life for myself. So, I did. I eventually made enough money to pay tuition for FIT, and I started there. I kept telling myself it wasn't bad what I was doing. *Everybody does it*, I told myself. *If I don't, then someone else will.* These people, most of them, wanted to go. They didn't know what awaited them once they got here. Usually, it was working in a field or a factory; for some, it was prostitution, but for most of them, I truly believed they were given a better future. I told myself I was helping them. They wanted to go. Or they wouldn't be willing to pay all that money for us to take them on a dangerous trip across the ocean. They knew the risks it involved. That's how I justified it for myself. But I was suffering. Deep inside, I was hurting. Seeing these people getting stowed away, hundreds of them in small compartments, was awful. So that's why I started doing drugs. I met a guy at FIT who introduced me to crack, and I took it without even questioning. Here was finally something that gave me peace, something that made me at ease and made me forget. And for about a year or so, I was doing great. I flew back and forth between Santo Domingo and Miami once or twice a month. I kept them on a schedule and made sure they paid our people in Miami and didn't keep the money for themselves. I ran a tight ship, and no one dared to defy me. When I went back there, I drove a big car. I was the queen of the island, and no longer a victim. I felt important. People knew who I was, and they respected me. It felt good. But once I was back on American soil, it didn't feel good anymore, and the more drugs I took to subdue it, the more I messed up. I was thrown out of FIT, and soon they found someone else to run the trafficking operation for them. I was cast out and found myself on the streets once again, alone and with no money, only craving my next fix. That's how fast it can go."

She sighed and placed a hand on my arm.

"Then, I met you—my savior. You picked me up in an abandoned house down in Overtown, where I had been living for months. I barely knew what year it was. You took me to rehab and paid out of your own pocket. No one had ever been so good to me. You came to see me every day and showed me so much love, it was overwhelming. I had never had anyone love me like that before. So, I decided to leave my past behind, and, once we got married, I believed it would actually happen. I was finally living the dream. When your colleagues, Wolfe and Ferdinand, realized who you were going to marry, they got scared. They came here, came to our house shortly after we married, when you weren't there, and threatened me. They told me if I ever said anything to you, they'd kill our daughter and me. I promised them I wouldn't. They came by at least once a year to make sure I wasn't talking, throwing all kinds of threats around and humiliating me, telling me what scum I was, what a whore I was, and that no one would believe me anyway. They said they'd let me take the fall, and I'd go away for the rest of my life. Stuff like that."

I looked up at Camille. I had listened while looking mostly at the floor below, my heart pounding in my chest.

"So, why did they try to kill you three years ago? What changed?" I asked, my voice shaking. I felt so repulsed by what I had heard; it was hard even to speak.

Camille exhaled. Her eyes filled and a tear escaped, then ran down her cheek.

"My brother came. He came to my door five years ago. After that, everything changed."

"Your brother? He was here?"

She nodded, closing her eyes briefly. "He said I owed him money. He had brought a couple of guys, and they threatened to reveal that I was an illegal immigrant if I didn't pay up. I had made it to America because of him, he said."

"But it wasn't him?" I asked. "He didn't bring you here?"

"Doesn't matter. He wanted money. So…I…well, I only know one way to get money…"

Camille looked away.

My hand slid out of hers, and I felt myself recoil.

"So, you…went back?"

She nodded, closing her eyes, tears streaming down her cheeks.

"I contacted Ferdinand, and he got me working the malls here, finding girls. I told him that's what I was good at, finding the girls that were broken. They trusted me, I told him. It was easy for me to get to them. They always walked with me willingly. So, I started working for him again and gave all the money I earned to my brother. It was tormenting me, but I couldn't see any other way out."

I stood to my feet, pushing the chair across the floor behind me, making a screeching sound.

"You…you were out of it. We had a great life and still you…went back to…that?" I could barely get the words across my lips. "We had everything, Camille, and still you…I can't believe you. Why didn't you come to me? Why didn't you ever tell me anything?"

"Don't you understand? I couldn't. Not only would they kill me and perhaps my family back in Santo Domingo, but I would also…lose you. You'd look at me the way you are now and yell at me like you just did. And I would lose Josie. I couldn't bear that. I was finally happy. I thought I could stop at any time, that I could just tell Ferdinand I was done once I had paid my debt, but they wouldn't let me. When I told them I was done, I wanted out because it was tormenting me to be lying to you, they came to our house one afternoon. They broke in through the back door, then injected me with drugs so I overdosed. They knew my story and knew to make it look like I was just some addict who had slipped. But they hadn't counted on me surviving. And now, they're trying to kill me again. These people, Harry…You don't know what you're up against. They're dangerous and powerful. There's no stopping them. They're everywhere."

I stared at her, my nostrils flaring violently, my fists clenched. I could feel pain in my jaw and realized I had bitten down so hard that it was hurting me.

"I...I can't believe this," I said, going back and forth inside the room.

Camille was crying heavily, sobbing, and I felt nothing. I couldn't make myself feel sorry for her, even if I tried. She had chosen this. She had made the choice for her and for us. She had exploited young, innocent girls and sent them into prostitution—sent them to slavery. She could justify it all she wanted. She could tell herself it was okay, that everyone did it, that these people wanted a better life, that she was helping them fulfill their dreams. She could say that she had no choice as much as she wanted to, but the fact was that these were nothing but excuses. She did have a choice. She had a choice back in the Dominican Republic, and she had a choice here. She most certainly had a choice after marrying me. Yet she still went back to it, and that made me angrier than anything.

How could I ever look into her eyes again and feel anything but disgust?

How could I ever forgive her?

"There might be no way of stopping them," I said, pointing at her. "But you're gonna help me do it anyway. Even if it costs us our lives. It's the only way for you to redeem yourself; do you hear me? You and me, we're taking them down, all of them. You're gonna tell the FBI everything you just told me. You're gonna give them names; you hear me? You're gonna give them all the names they need, leaving no one out. If you ever want to see Josie again, that's how it'll go down. Are we clear?"

Chapter 33

JEAN COULDN'T SLEEP. It wasn't exactly a surprise. How could anyone sleep after what had happened? After seeing a drive-by shooting of your neighbor's house, of the man you loved, fearing for his and his family's lives. After saving Camille's life, fighting to stop the bleeding, then rushing her to the hospital? No one would be able to sleep after that.

The fear still lingered in her throat and felt like a lump. Jean realized she wasn't going to get any sleep, so she got up and walked downstairs to the kitchen, where she grabbed herself a glass of water, then went to the freezer and pulled out a bucket of Ben and Jerry's. She ate it with a spoon while looking into the street, tears running down her cheeks, her hand shaking as she dug the spoon into the ice cream.

It didn't help, though. Not as much as she wanted it to. She still felt terrible, and there was nothing that seemed to make her feel better. There was only one thing left to do.

She grabbed her phone and called her sister. Anna

didn't pick up till her third try when a sleepy voice sounded on the other end.

"Jean? Is something wrong?"

"I'm sorry for calling like this," Jean said. "I know you were sleeping. I just needed someone to talk to."

"Hold on. Give me a sec. I'm going down to the kitchen, so we don't wake up the kids. Okay, I'm here now. I'm all yours. What's going on? You're scaring me, sis. You never call like this."

Jean grabbed another spoonful and plopped it in her mouth.

"Is that ice cream?" her sister asked. "Is it that bad?"

"It's worse."

"It's him again, isn't it? Harry, right? I've told you he's bad news, sweetie. He'll never leave his wife, and you're gonna end up hurt. I've said this from the beginning."

"I know. I know. It's just that…today was really bad."

"What happened?"

"Someone tried to kill Harry and his family. A drive-by shooting. I watched it all from my house. I was so scared, Anna, you have no idea."

Anna shrieked at the other end.

"A drive-by shooting? Are you kidding me? Tell me it isn't true. I always said Miami was a dangerous place for you. I never liked you living there, but geez. I'm telling you this because I love you, Jean. You need to listen to me. You have got to get out of that town."

"I knew you'd say that," she said. "I'm still thinking about it. Like we talked about the other day. I'm looking at listings and have applied for a couple of positions in your area."

"No, nah-ah. We can't wait for that," she said, getting her big sister tone on. "You've got to move faster than that. Tomorrow, Jean. Tomorrow you pack up a few things, and then you drive up here. We'll send for the rest of your things. I don't care that they need you at the hospital or that Harry needs you. You have to get away now. You come up here. We'll find you a place to live and a job. You can stay with me, Mike, and the kids till you find something else. We have a guest room; you know this. I'm not asking, Jean. I'm telling you to do this now. Are you listening?"

Jean nodded, pressing the phone closer to her ear. She loved her sister so dearly and couldn't understand why she had lived so far apart from her for so many years. Why had it taken her so long to realize how important family was?

"Okay," she said with a sniffle. "I'll come."

"Tomorrow."

"Tomorrow."

She hung up, feeling slightly invigorated. This was a good thing. This was the right thing. Now was as good a time as ever. She could start over. It was possible to forget and move on.

Jean stared out the window at Harry's house next to hers, then exhaled, thinking about what it could have been, but never was.

We came so close, Harry. So close.

Then she went upstairs, found her old suitcase, and started packing. She was going to leave first thing in the morning. She might as well, she figured. Just call the hospital and tell them she quit—that she was leaving town.

Would she tell Harry?

You don't owe him anything.

Still, she'd sent him an email. Yes, she'd do that. Or a text. A text was a little more personal. She'd thank him for all he had been for her and tell him it was time they both moved on, then wish him luck. She had all the sentences ready in her mind and knew exactly how to write it. She carried the suitcase down by the door, so it was ready for the morning. Anna was right. She could send for her things later.

Then, she sat down and started writing the text to Harry, trying to frame it properly, wondering how exactly one said goodbye to the man you loved when you were still in love with him.

That's when the phone rang. When it was still between her hands, and she had written the first words,

Dear Harry…

His name appeared on the display, and her heart sank.

Why was he calling her now? It had to be important, she thought, then picked up.

He sounded agitated and maybe a little scared. His breathing had a desperate sound to it.

"Jean? I'm so glad you picked up. I was afraid you wouldn't."

"Harry? What…"

"Oh, Jean," he said, sounding almost like he was crying. "I need you. I'm so sorry to call you like this, but I really, *really* need you right now."

Jean closed her eyes and exhaled deeply. Her sister's words rang in her head from back when she realized Jean was taking care of him and his wife, who was in a vegetative state. Jean had told her she was just helping out a little bit until they got into the routine—until they got things figured out. It was just for a month or two tops, she had told her, even though she knew it wasn't true, even if part of her hoped it would be longer.

"He'll never stop asking you to do stuff, and he'll only pay you back with a wounded heart. You won't be able to say no to him because you're in love with him, and he'll end up hurting you even worse. Break it off now. Make it fast. Less pain that way."

Make it fast.

"Harry…I…" Jean began.

"She told me everything," he said, crying, breaking down.

Jean held her breath. She couldn't stand even the thought of Harry crying. It broke her heart to pieces. She loved him too much to ignore him being sad.

"Camille did?" she asked, surprised. This wasn't what she had expected.

"Yes," he said. "Please, Jean. I don't know what to do with myself. I'm a mess. I need you."

She exhaled, biting her lip, a million voices in her head were telling her not to do this, that it would only end badly.

"Stay where you are. I'll be right there."

Chapter 34

I LEFT Camille at the hospital. I couldn't stay in that room with her anymore. I couldn't be anywhere near her. I met with Jean in the parking lot, and I got into her car. We drove back to her house in silence, while I stared out the window, trying to gather myself at least enough to be able to tell Jean everything.

I waited until we were in her house, drinking coffee at her kitchen table. Then I told her everything Camille had told me, every last detail. I needed to get it out. I guess it was a way for me to digest it, to talk about it, and let it sink in properly. I also needed her to understand. I needed her to realize that Camille and I were over. There was no way I could stay with her.

I was done.

"Wow," Jean said when I finally stopped talking and both of our coffees were almost gone. "For real?"

"For real," I said, nodding slowly. "I'm not making this up. I mean, you can't really make up something like this. But it makes a lot of sense to me now. She never wanted to talk about her past or her family. When I asked, she'd brush me off quickly and turn to something else. I just assumed she had a terrible relationship with her parents or something, or she was embarrassed about her background. I could never have imagined this. And then, later on, she was always so secretive when I asked her what she had been doing all day. I kept asking her if she didn't want to go back to school, if she wasn't bored at the house after Josie had started school, and she just said she kept herself busy. Now, I know with what." I chuckled angrily at that last part. I still could hardly believe this story, or that I had been such a fool.

"Luring young girls into slavery?" Jean asked, fingers tapping on the side of her cup. "I can't believe it. I thought I knew Camille. This is insane."

"Now, you know how I feel."

Jean looked up, and our eyes met. "I am sorry, Harry. This must feel awful. I can't even imagine…"

"I am done with her," I said, locking with Jean's eyes and not letting go. "I can't go back. Not after this."

Jean swallowed. Her eyes scrutinized mine. Then she nodded swiftly. "I can't blame you. This is a lot to take in, for anyone."

I took Jean's hand in mine. We both looked down at our hands, then I leaned forward, grabbed her face between my hands, and pulled her into a kiss. The kiss was soft and gentle and absolutely wonderful. It was all I had dreamt of and even more. And for the first time, it didn't fill me with this deep nagging sensation of guilt because I had nothing to feel guilty about anymore.

I was free. I was finally free to love Jean.

"Harry…I…," she whispered as our lips parted.

"Shh," I said. My forehead was leaning against hers. Her breath was on my skin. I didn't want to talk anymore. I wanted to enjoy the moment, make it last. When I opened my eyes to look at her, they fell on something behind her. Something standing in the living room next to the front door that I hadn't noticed when we walked in, but now I did. Now, it was all I could see.

"What's that?"

I pulled away abruptly.

"What's what…?"

She turned to look, then sank into her chair.

"A suitcase?" I asked, my voice trembling slightly as the realization sank in. At first, I told myself that she could, after all, just be going on a short trip to see her family or just a vacation, even though I knew she rarely did that, if ever. But as I turned my head, I saw papers in a stack on the kitchen counter, close to where I was sitting, close enough for me to see what they were.

"And listings? Those look like rental listings and job listings for…" I leaned over and looked closer. "Savannah?"

"Harry…I…"

I looked at her, startled. "You're leaving? For good?"

"Well…not just yet…"

"But soon, right? The suitcase is by the door. It's all packed, right? You were going to leave in the morning, weren't you? Just leave us without saying a word? Not even a goodbye?"

"I was going to tell you."

Jean reached over and removed the stack of papers, putting them in a drawer, trying to hide them. But it was too late.

"It's nothing," she said.

"Nothing? You were planning on leaving. That's not nothing."

"I am sorry."

"But… How? How will I survive without you?" I

asked, suddenly feeling hopeless. "You…you can't leave us, Jean."

"That's not fair, Harry. I need a life too," she said with a sniffle, then walked to the window, turning her back on me. "I need to move on."

I looked down. It all seemed so futile now. What was I even doing here? Why was I spilling my guts out to Jean when she was about to leave?

I rose to my feet and grabbed my phone from the table.

"I'll let you go then. I understand."

I walked to the door. She turned around.

"Harry, I…"

I paused, hand on the doorknob.

"No, Jean, I haven't been fair to you. You're right. I need to sort out my mess on my own from now on. I wish you luck and hope you'll be very happy up there. Believe me, I do want the best for you, and this is it. I'm not good for you; I'm trouble."

I stormed out the door before I could break down and cry, then rushed to my own house, ducking under the crime scene tape, and walked inside where all the bullet holes were marked with numbers, tears running down my cheeks, wondering how I could have been such a darn fool. I had thought she'd wait for me forever. But of course, she couldn't. Now, I didn't understand why I thought she would. How had I not seen what I was doing to her, how she was hurting in all this?

I had been so selfish.

Chapter 35

I STAYED UPSTAIRS ALL NIGHT, wandering about in my bedroom. Every now and then, I daydreamed, looking towards Jean's house, thinking about what could have been, but for the most part, I researched. I dove right into working on the case to keep me from thinking about Jean and how much I had screwed up…how I hadn't realized time was running out.

I sighed and went through the autopsy of Kate Taylor once again, looking closely at the details that I had wondered about earlier, that frankly had startled me quite a lot. I still couldn't figure out the pieces, how they were connected, but there was something here that didn't add up.

I walked to the window and looked down into the street. Part of the area in front of our house had been blocked off, and a piece of crime scene tape was blowing in the wind. The crime scene techs had worked until late and would be back the next morning to finish, they had told me. I knew me being in the house was tampering with the scene of a crime, and I wasn't supposed to be there at all, but I didn't know where else to go, and I needed my computer and files to do my work. I would make sure to be out of there by the time the crime scene bus arrived in the morning.

Staying in my old house wasn't exactly comfortable, and I wondered if I would ever live here again. It had been our house, mine and Camille's house that we bought together. There had been so many happy moments shared here. And now it felt like it had all been a lie.

Was none of it real?

Once we started the process of the divorce, we'd have to figure out all those things. Did we keep the house? Did I simply buy her out and stay here with Josie? Or did we sell it and split the money? I still loved this house, and it was Josie's childhood home, but after tonight, I wasn't sure we'd ever be happy here again.

Especially not if Jean wasn't our neighbor anymore.

I also wondered what would happen to Camille. I was going to bring Agent Jackson to her tomorrow so she could tell her story to him and give him the information he needed, especially the names. The FBI would most likely cut a deal with her if she promised to testify against them. But would they try to kill her again? And would she have to serve time herself?

Probably.

I sighed and thought about Josie and how she'd once again have to miss her mother. We'd share custody, so that once she got out, Josie would be with her half of the time, if Josie wasn't an adult already and could choose for herself when to see either of us. The thought terrified me. How would she ever survive in this brutal world? Would it eat her up like it had her mother?

I shook my head and decided I didn't want to think about it. Instead, I thought about my visit with Nick Taylor and then his father, Andrew Taylor, and how angry he and been when addressing me. Why did the boy tell me to ask his new wife? Was he just a typical angry teenager trying to get his new stepmom in trouble? Because he hated her? Or what did he mean?

I sat down at the computer, then did my research. It didn't take me long to find tons of information about Andrew Taylor, the State Attorney.

As I scrolled down all my hits, I came across a picture from his wedding with his second wife. I couldn't believe what I was looking at. I couldn't believe *who* I was looking at. But seeing this, everything suddenly made a whole lot of sense.

I had finally found my missing piece.

As I pondered this new information, my phone buzzed in my pocket, and I pulled it out.

An unknown number usually meant it was Al.

Chapter 36

I WAS WAITING OUTSIDE of Fowler's office as he came to work the next morning. He stopped when he saw me, jaw almost dropped.

"Hunter? Are you okay? I heard what happened last night. What are you even doing here?"

"I had something important to tell you. I've solved the murder of Kate Taylor."

Fowler lifted his bushy eyebrows. "That old thing? It's ten years old, Harry."

"But never closed. I know who did it. Let me show you."

We walked inside, and I didn't sit down for once. Instead, I spread out all my papers, opened all the files, and started to explain it all to him, going into each and every detail. I told him my plan and how to take down the killer, then left in a hurry. I drove to the hospital, where I met with FBI Agent Jackson outside in the parking lot.

We shook hands, then walked inside, where I showed him to Camille's room. I listened in as she told him everything, every little detail about the trafficking ring and her own part of it, making sure she got it all out, even how deeply involved she had been. The agent recorded everything and took notes while she spoke. I was very pleased with how thorough she was. Most of the names she threw on the table were no surprise to me, but some of them most certainly were.

"And you'll testify to all this?" Agent Jackson said as she had finished.

She nodded. "Yes."

"And you do realize this means you're incriminating yourself as well, right?" he asked.

Camille closed her eyes and nodded again.

"Yes."

"We can probably ask the DA to look for a reduced sentence and get you a good deal," he added, "if you show up in court and tell them these things you've told me today."

She swallowed. She was exhausted, but the doctor had said she was well enough to do this. I wanted to strike while she was still willing to talk, fearing she might regret it if we waited too long.

"We could also apply to get you into the witness protection program," he said.

Camille's eyes landed on mine.

"But...Josie?"

"You wouldn't see her again," I said.

"Or she'd have to go with her," Agent Jackson said.

I shook my head. "I am not losing my daughter too."

"You are married. You could both go," he said. "You could start over in a safer place."

The thought was appealing. It really was. Right now, there wasn't anything that made me want to stay in Miami. But I couldn't leave my job, and I couldn't move somewhere else and start a new life with the wife I didn't love anymore. It was simply not possible.

Agent Jackson gathered his things and rose to his feet. "Think about it…both of you. Once this is over, you'll have made a lot of enemies. It might not even be a choice anymore. It might be a necessity."

ONE WEEK LATER

Chapter 37

"YOU READY FOR THIS?"

Fowler looked at me. He was wearing his Kevlar vest the same as I was, along with a helmet. We both had our weapons in our hands.

"It's not every day you get to take down a murderer," he continued.

I nodded, feeling satisfied, yet still nervous, as was typical in the situation. We had no idea what the outcome would be. Hopefully, we'd get the killer, and no one needed to be hurt.

But that wasn't always how these things panned out, unfortunately.

"I'm ready."

Fowler grinned. "Then, let's do it. Perimeter is set up; we have the house surrounded. Let's go."

Fowler went in first, and I followed. We found him in the living room.

"Police!" Fowler yelled. "Hands where I can see them."

Andrew Taylor was on the floor fast, arms over his head, wearing his PJs. A cup of coffee was on the floor and had spilled the black substance in a puddle, ruining the nice beige carpet. It was Saturday morning, and he had probably thought he'd be able to enjoy his morning coffee in peace and quiet.

I wasn't sorry to have ruined that.

"Andrew Taylor," I said. "You're under arrest for the murder of Kate Taylor. You have the right to remain silen…"

"What's going on here?"

The woman at the top of the stairs looked down at us, her eyes were petrified. I smiled and pointed my gun at her.

"Just the person we were looking for. Would you please come down here, ma'am? Slowly and keep those hands above your head, where I can see them, please."

"But…"

She did as she was told and walked down with her hands stretched above her head.

"What are you people doing here? What are you doing to my husband?"

As she approached me, I smiled again. "We're arresting him. For the murder of his ex-wife. Or rather for conspiracy to. Because he didn't exactly kill her himself, did he? You did that."

Her eyes met mine. I saw confusion in them and defiance. "I…"

"Save it," I said. "We know you did it."

"Don't say anything, Joan," Andrew Taylor said.

"I don't intend to," she said, walking closer to me, looking into my eyes.

Those were the last words said before we dragged them away. We let them sweat it out for few hours before they were taken into an interrogation room, Fowler and I doing the interrogation together.

"I didn't do anything," Andrew said. "I had nothing to do with it."

"Okay," I said, placing the files on the desk in front of them, then taking out the pictures of Kate Taylor from when she was pulled out of the water. I placed them so they couldn't avoid looking at them. "Then tell me about Kate. I'd like to hear about her from both of you."

Neither of them said anything. Not that it was a surprise.

"Okay. Let's do this another way. I tell you how I think it all went down, and then you can stop me if I got it wrong, okay?"

I looked first at one, then the other. No one said anything.

"I need my lawyer," Andrew Taylor said. "I'm not saying anything until he gets here."

"Of course not," I said. "Until then, I'll just talk a little bit if you don't mind. You can always correct me if I get things wrong."

They didn't make a sound.

"So, when did you two start seeing one another?" I continued. "When did you fall in love? When did your affair start?"

Still nothing.

"See, I have a feeling you planned this for a very long time, didn't you? Because you had fallen in love, you and Andrew. But Kate didn't want to give you a divorce, am I right? So, you wanted to get rid of her. It was easily planned once you got started. Joan invited her to celebrate her birthday with your third friend, Kristin, thinking it was a great alibi. Especially since you chose a weekend where Andrew was at a conference in Atlanta, providing him with a rock-solid alibi, and he would be the first suspect. We all know that. And it went down perfectly. No one suspected foul play from her good friends. But what got to me first was the fact that no one had seen Kate with you down there. When interviewed afterward, the bartender said he remembered seeing both you and Kristin, but not Kate. Now, the investigation was mostly focused on that guy, Matt, and finding him, and no one had seen him either. None of the guests in the bar or anyone working there had seen them. Not Kate nor Matt. And it took me a while to figure it out, but I realized that Matt doesn't even exist. Kristin panicked, didn't she? When she was interviewed by the police, she thought she should come up with something better than what you had planned. So, she made up some guy Kate might have met, someone the police could focus on investigating, a possible killer. But since it wasn't planned, you didn't talk about him until the detective mentioned him, realizing Kristin had to have talked about him. During the rest of the interview, both of your stories were a complete match, a little too much, to be honest. Using the same sentences, like she needed to *blow off some steam*, or she *wanted to disappear*, she was *bummed out about her marriage*, stuff like that was the same, word for word. And that smells like you two talked it over beforehand, getting your stories straight. But Matt was only in Kristin's memory because she made him up while sitting there at the sheriff's office, thinking it would be better, it would be more plausible if she painted a picture of Kate as being loose, as wanting to sleep with another guy, and then maybe he could have killed her. It was a better story than her simply vanishing out of the blue like you first planned, hoping they'd think it was suicide. But the fact was, no one had seen Kate in Key West because she wasn't there. She was somewhere else, wasn't she? She was suffering a slow and painful death."

Chapter 38

THE ROOM WAS EERILY QUIET. The two of them didn't even move, barely blinked. Not even a raised eyebrow.

"Anyone have anything to add?" I asked, sipping my cup of coffee, praying their lawyer wasn't going to burst in anytime soon. Fowler was staring at them, leaned back in his chair, letting me run the show.

"No? You don't have anything to say for yourself?"

I put the cup down, my eyes lingering on both of them.

Finally, Andrew Taylor lifted his eyes and met mine. "It wasn't like that. You don't understand."

"Oh, really? Then tell me. What did I miss?"

A look from Joan made him lean back and clam up.

"Okay," I said. I placed my fists on the table and leaned forward, getting close to Andrew Taylor.

"Then, let's try this. She hurt your son. That's why you did it."

The look in Andrew's eyes told me I was on track.

"See, at first I assumed it was you who did it, that you had abused Nick. But then I realized that it stopped. There were no more reports, and when I called the school, they said it had stopped after DCF was put on the case. After that, Nick never had bruises again. Because his mom was dead. Kate was the one who tortured your son, wasn't she?" I continued. "And you knew you could never get her out of your life otherwise. DCF had been involved, but they dismissed the case. How could you make anyone else understand what was going on if they wouldn't? They'd only think you were the one abusing him because let's face it; it's more likely the father would do such a thing."

Andrew leaned forward. "I didn't know how bad it was until DCF told me what Nick had said. The details of how she made him lick the toilet and cut himself were unbearable. I had to do something at least. After DCF dismissed the case, I tried to solve it myself. I kept an eye on her when she was alone with him. I went out of my way to make sure they weren't alone. One day, I walked in on her as she pushed his head into the toilet bowl and flushed. That's when I knew I had to do something. But I didn't have the guts. Not till I asked Joan for help and told her about it. She suggested it; she suggested we get rid of her."

Joan let out a small angry snort, and Andrew gave her a look, then bowed his head. "They know," he mumbled. "It's not like I'm telling them anything they don't already know."

"Just stop," she grumbled.

I continued. "So, she came up with how it could be done. Because after her divorce, Joan had gone back to working again, back at the hyperbaric treatment clinic where she worked before she married her first husband, who didn't want you to work, am I right? That's where I met you when I brought in Camille. But your name is Joan Kendrick now, not Joan Smith, like the woman in the files, the one who reported her best friend missing. You took your maiden name after the divorce. And you never took

Andrew's last name since you tried that once when you were married before, and it was too much trouble to change your name once again. That's why I never made the connection. Not until now, at least. So, here's what I believe happened. You chose a weekend Andrew would be away at a conference in Atlanta, and his alibi would be solid since he would be the first one they looked at. You don't have to watch a lot of crime shows or even be the State Attorney to know this. You brought Kristin along. She was your best friend. You could trust her. You told Kate you could help her with something she had trouble with. I found her medical records and realized she was diabetic, and she had a foot ulcer that wouldn't go away— a type of condition many people came to your clinic and received treatment for. You promised her free treatment if she came on the weekend, out of normal operating hours. She crawled inside the chamber, and you turned it on. And then you simply just left her there, knowing no one else would come in all weekend when the clinic was closed. I read the autopsy, and that's when it occurred to me that she hadn't drowned. Her eardrums were popped, and there was permanent scarring, called fibrosis of the lung tissue, a symptom of oxygen toxicity that can lead to death, as you yourself have taught me. You also taught me that it is one of the side effects of being inside a hyperbaric chamber for too long. It was a risk, you said. So, I thought, what about an entire weekend? What if she was left in there for two whole days? Knocking on the sides, suffering, screaming for help, but no one hearing her? Unable to get out? After that, you could have taken her dead body out, driven her down to Key West, where you placed her in the water, making it look like she drowned. Then you went to the police station and told them your friend had gone missing, after making sure your stories were straight. What I can't figure out is why Kristin was willing to go along with it."

I saw a hint of a frown between Joan's eyes.

"Unless…" I said, scrutinizing her. "Unless she had something…" I flipped a few pages and returned to the initial interview with her. "Kristin wasn't married. Why was that? Did it have something to do with Kate?"

Joan's nostrils were flaring, and I could tell I was getting closer.

"What did Kate do?" I asked. "What did she do to Kristin?"

"She slept with him, okay?" Joan said, spurting it out. She was like a pressure cooker that had finally reached its limits. "Kristin had met this sweet guy that she really liked, and Kate kept telling her that he'd cheat on her. When Kristin came home and found the two of them in bed together, all she could say was: I told you so. That's the kind of woman she was."

"But that wasn't all, was it?" I asked. "There has to have been more for you both actually to want to kill her."

Joan sighed deeply.

"What did she do to you? You've all known each other since college. What did she do that made you want to kill her to revenge yourselves?"

Joan swallowed. I could tell she was debating with herself what to say next. She wanted to tell me; I could see it in her eyes. She wanted to justify herself. As I stared into her eyes, it suddenly occurred to me. There was a detail I had missed. Her eyes. Her piercing green eyes.

"Oh, dear Lord," I said. "Nick is your son, isn't he? He's not Kate's?"

That's when she finally broke down and cried—leaning forward, mouth half-open, her upper body convulsing.

"Kate couldn't have children of her own," I said.

"Sh-she forced me to give him to her. When I got pregnant."

"Because he was Andrew's child. Because you had an affair with Andrew. Why did you agree to it, Joan?"

"Andrew persuaded me and told me it was best for the child. I know now he only did it out of fear of Kate. They'd raise the child like it was theirs, they said. I had recently married and didn't want an affair to destroy everything, so I agreed to it, even though it was the hardest thing I have ever done. I told my husband I was doing an internship overseas for nine months, then left. Kate and Andrew came over and took the baby home. I came back different. I never became the same woman again. And for all these years, I had to watch him grow up with her as a mother. It was pure torture."

"And then when you realized that the abuse was happening, you knew you had to get rid of her. But it wasn't that easy. DCF believed her and not the child, and she refused to give Andrew a divorce. She would take Nick with her, and then you'd lose him completely."

"The woman was insane," Andrew said. "You must understand this. She was abusive to anyone in her proximity. It was impossible to get out of her claws. It was her friends, her family; all experienced her evilness. She was nothing but pure evil. She'd even cut herself to make it look like I was abusing her. She'd hurt herself to make her friends feel sorry for her and think I was the bad guy. I would even see her do it. Once, we were having a fight, and she grabbed a knife and cut herself on the throat, then yelled that she'd call the police and tell them I did it. I know how the system works. The police would have to arrest me no matter what I told them, and the press would be all over it. I didn't have the guts to leave her. She'd ruin my life, she said. Make sure I never saw Nick again.

Destroy my career by telling the world I had abused Nick and was a child molester. I'm the Miami-Dade County State Attorney. It would have ruined me. She had the power to destroy me completely, and she would have done so if I hadn't stopped her. She would have completely ruined my son too, and I couldn't let her do that."

"But he was already damaged. You realized it when you found the videos on his computer," I said. "That's why you wanted him to stay behind bars. You feared he'd become like his mother. He had been abused, and now he was abusing others. It was better for you if he stayed there —if he went to jail. You were scared of what he might do if he got out."

"I told you he was a liar. Just like his mother, he manipulated and lied constantly. When he pulled that gun out in church, it was just part of his show. He wanted you to think I was abusing him, but in fact, he was abusing others. I had told him the night before that I'd go to the police with what I had found, showing them how he had humiliated those girls, that's why he brought the gun. To take me down, not to kill me. But to make it look like he had no other way. He was going down and dragging me down with him. That was his plan. And I guess he succeeded. I never told him the truth about who his birth mother was. There never really was the right time." Andrew glanced at Joan briefly. "He hated her guts, and it tormented her daily. Now, I guess it's too late. It's simply too late."

"It is, for both of you," I said.

I closed the file, then stopped the recording. I folded my hands with a deep sigh. "I think I've heard enough."

"Me too," Fowler said, then rose to his feet.

As he walked to the door, he shared a look with Andrew Taylor that for a second made me think they knew one another, but then it was gone.

Chapter 39

WE STAYED at my dad's place, further down the street. Our house was still a crime scene, and to be honest, I wasn't sure I'd ever feel comfortable there again. I considered selling it once it was all over, but who'd want to buy a house full of bullet holes? One way or another, I'd have to fix it up first. And I really didn't want to.

I hadn't seen Camille for several days. She was taken into the FBI's custody as soon as she was released from the hospital, and I didn't know where they were keeping her. If we'd ever see her again, I didn't know either. For me, it wouldn't matter much, but for Josie, it still did.

My dad had made spaghetti and meatballs for us, and we sat around the table, eating in silence.

"I solved my case today," I said and took a second portion.

"Really?" my dad said. "Well done."

"We got a full confession and everything. Three people were involved in planning it. We have two of them; the third will be taken in tomorrow, and we'll need her confession too. But it looks like we'll be able to close it soon."

"I bet that feels good," my dad said and leaned back. "Serving God by serving the people."

"It does," I said. "Even though it's never as black and white as you'd like it to be."

"You mean the murderer is actually human?" he asked.

I chuckled. "Yeah, something like that. I always want them to be these vicious, mean people that belong behind bars. But they're never that. Still need to do their time, though. I don't feel bad about it."

"But you're human too," he said. "So, you understand them."

"I don't really understand them killing a person, but I guess I understand their pain if you know what I mean. I don't know. Is anyone having more? I can eat the rest if no one else can."

Josie shook her head. She had her phone under the table and was obviously not very present because of it. She thought I didn't see it, and I pretended not to. I didn't want us to fight. Not tonight. She had been through so much the past few months and years, even with her mother being sick and all. I could cut her some slack.

"So, Josie, any plans for the weekend?" I asked. "Josie?"

She looked up from her phone. I smiled, and she put it away, looking embarrassed. "The weekend? It's only Thursday, Dad."

She said it in that teenage way like I didn't even know that it was Thursday.

"I know, and I wanted to ask you first because I wanted us to do something together this weekend."

She made a face. "Something? Like what? Please don't say something lame like going to the Everglades. I hate that place. Or the beach. I can't stand all that sand. It gets everywhere."

"It's nothing like that," I said. "I thought maybe we could go swim with dolphins in Key Largo. I know you've always wanted to do that."

Josie's eyes grew huge. She dropped the fork from her hand. She let out a small shriek. "Really? I thought it was too expensive? You always said it was?"

"It is, but I think we deserve it, don't we?"

"Oh, my God, Dad. Are you being serious right now? I have dreamt about this since I was a baby."

"I know you have," I said. "And now, it's time. Now, do your homework."

Josie almost danced up the stairs to the temporary bedroom my dad had given her. I smiled and turned to look at him, sitting next to me.

"Feeling pretty good about yourself there, aren't ya'?" he asked.

"Yes, as a matter of fact, I am feeling good about this. I always wanted to take Josie down there, to this rescue center where they take care of injured dolphins and where you can get in the water with them. It's extremely expensive, but I think it's worth it."

My dad nodded. "And it certainly isn't a way for you to buy her happiness because she might never see her mom again? Or a way for you to create a diversion, so you won't have to tell her?"

"Maybe," I said.

"Don't you think you owe it to her to talk to her about it, at least? To tell her the truth?"

I swallowed. "How can I? I'm not about to tell her what her mom has done. It would break her heart."

"True, but it will break her heart either way. If her mom takes the witness protection program or goes to jail, either way, she'll be out of her life. She needs to know."

I grabbed my plate and rose to my feet with an

annoyed movement. My dad was right, as always, but I didn't want him to be. If I wanted to take my daughter swimming with dolphins to avoid questions about her mother, then so be it. That was my issue, not his.

Chapter 40

I WAS FEELING PRETTY confident and good about myself as I entered the station the next morning. Josie had been the happiest girl all morning, and I had to admit I was enjoying seeing her like this for once. Ever since the shooting incident, she had been so down and sad, and she had slept terribly at night. Most nights, I had slept with her, to be there and hold her when she had nightmares. This night was the first that she slept through without even waking up. It gave me hope that she'd get past this too. I had found her a therapist that she was going to see for the first time today since I wasn't sure I could deal with it all by myself.

I sat down at my desk, then opened my computer, ready to finish my report on the Kate Taylor murder, but for some reason, I couldn't find it. I searched the entire database, but it simply wasn't there. All there was, was the old case file from Key West; none of my work was anywhere to be seen.

I was starting to sweat now, and my hands were getting

clammy as I searched for the audio file from the interrogation.

It wasn't there either.

It was gone.

Vanished.

"What in the…?"

I kept searching, going through everything, my fingers tapping the keyboard, my heart pounding in my chest, but still, nothing turned up. No results, it said. I then walked to the cabinet behind my desk to find the paper version that I always kept there.

It was gone too.

"What the…?"

I turned around to look at my desk, but I hadn't left it there either. I searched my bag, my drawers, everywhere.

Nothing.

All that was left were the old case files. It was like I had never done any work on this case at all.

What is this? I can't believe it?

I called down to the detention center and asked if they still had Andrew Taylor in custody.

"He was released last night," the woman said.

Released? He hadn't been to court yet; he couldn't have had a judge set bail yet?

"And Joan Kendrick?"

"Also released."

"On what grounds?"

"Case was dismissed," she said. "Charges were dropped. That's all it says in the papers."

"Who signed the release form?" I asked, my voice shaking with anger and frustration. I couldn't for the life of me figure out what was going on, how this was possible. How could this have happened?

"That would be Abraham Fowler," she said. "Major Abraham Fowler."

Chapter 41

HE WAS on the phone when I rang the doorbell, and as he opened the door, he finished his conversation.

"I gotta call you back. There's something I need to deal with here," Fowler said, then hung up. He gave me a look. I couldn't tell if it was concern in his eyes or resentment.

"Hunter? What are you doing here?"

I pushed my way past him inside, and he closed the front door behind me. The amount of marble on the man's floors and walls gave the place a cold feel.

"You let them go?" I asked.

Fowler let out a deep sigh. "So, that's what this is about. I should have known. Please…Hunter, sit."

"Oh, I prefer to stand," I said.

"You're mad. I can't blame you. But you know how it is, Hunter."

I shook my head. "No, I don't. Not this one. We did everything correctly. We had a warrant when we went in. We Mirandised them properly. We had a full recorded confession. He admitted to conspiring to kill his wife. His new wife admitted to actually killing her. We had them both. Now, I hear that you let them go. Why?"

Fowler threw out his arms. "Because I couldn't let you take them down. At least not him. He's too important."

A frown emerged between my eyes. "Important? Because he's the Miami-Dade County State Attorney?"

Fowler's eyes met mine, and the dime finally dropped. I took a step backward, startled.

"You have got to be kidding me. You let him go because you needed him? Because he's part of it too? The trafficking ring. I should have known. A guy like him is very good to have on hand. He knows what's going on, but you pay him to look the other way. The very same person who is supposed to be trying to combat trafficking is on your payroll. Clever. You run that whole darn operation, don't you? I didn't want to believe you did; I didn't want to see it, but of course, you do. It makes a lot of sense. Now, you can't risk him being in custody since he might reveal what he knows. Maybe he'll even try and make a deal. Am I right?"

Fowler's expression changed. His eyes were angry now.

"Am I right?" I asked again, slamming my fist onto his kitchen counter. "At least be honest with me."

"Yes, you're right," Fowler said with a snort.

"I can't believe you," I said. "Those…young children, those families who were being transported…you did that? You made money off that?"

"It was good money, okay? More than that, it was millions. Man, Hunter, you have no idea how much money it was. And you could have been in on it if you hadn't been…well, you. Besides, we did them a favor. They wanted to come here; they wanted to come. We made that possible. If it hadn't been us, it would've been someone else. That's the way the world goes. It used to be drug trafficking that was the most lucrative around here, but this is where the money is. So, there will always be someone doing it, taking that money. Might as well be us. Don't you see?"

"You broke the law. Human trafficking is a serious offense, and you know this. You subjected those poor people to great danger. And what about the girls that were kidnapped, the ones Camille lured in, huh? What happened to them? Did they end up on the street somewhere, drugged out of their minds, and raped by hundreds of men? Did you ever stop to think about them?"

Fowler stared at me, his fists clenched. He was looking for something that could justify his actions, but not finding it.

"These people...your people tried to kill my family," I said.

"You kept getting in my way, Hunter. I tried to warn you. I tried to get you off our backs, but you kept coming back. The others wanted to get rid of you long ago, but I kept telling them you were harmless. I protected you, Hunter. People are pissed at you, and I can't hold them back anymore. I love you like a brother, Harry, but I'm afraid it ends here. I'm not letting you ruin what I spent years building up. I'm sorry you had to find yourself in the middle of all this, but it's pure business. You can't stop it now."

I looked down at him, the man I had known since we were both in our early twenties. I thought I knew him. I thought we were on the same side.

A smile spread from the corner of my lip.

"I'm sorry; I'm afraid I already have," I said.

"What?"

"No, wait...I'm not sorry," I added. With a swift movement, I pulled up my shirt so he could see the wire I was wearing.

Fowler went pale, his eyes blank.

"W-what?"

"Say hello to Agent Jackson from the FBI. He has been listening in for quite some time now, waiting for you finally to confess. Remember that microphone that you told me you had found in your office? Thinking it would lead me somehow to whoever put it up, I went to Al. She traced it for me, and the digital footprint led her directly to your computer. You made up that story about your office being bugged because you knew I suspected you when they found Josie, and you were the only one who knew where she was. But by giving me that tale about the microphone, you believed you had lied your way out of it. But the thing is, there's always a footprint, and Al found it. So, I went to Agent Jackson and told him my suspicion. Ever since, he's been listening in on all my conversations, especially with you. Camille then later confirmed our suspicion when she started naming names. Now, if we use the recordings from today, from right now, along with her testimony and the video my neighbor Jean recorded of you driving the car during that drive-by shooting, I think we have evidence enough to put you away for quite some time, don't you think?"

Fowler stared up at me. He didn't even blink and barely breathed.

"I can't believe you did that. I can't believe you'd do that to me. We were friends, Hunter. We were like family."

"I can't believe any of the stuff you've done, so I guess we're even," I said. "Now, I'm afraid I have to put you under arrest."

Fowler pulled out his gun and pointed it at me. I lifted my hands. Sweat was springing to his forehead.

"I can't let you do that, Hunter. Don't move! Don't come anywhere near me, or I will kill you."

"Whoa," I said and stepped back. "What do you think you're doing with that? The FBI is waiting right outside. They came here with me when I told them I was coming to see you. You wanna kill me and add murder to the list of crimes? You don't want to do that, Fowler. Don't be a fool."

He shook his head. He looked confused. "Stay where you are. Down on your knees and stay there."

I did as he told me. He then asked me to bend my head down, and I heard his footsteps move across the marble tiles, then a door slide open. A second later, I heard an engine start.

No!

The front door burst open, and Agent Jackson stepped inside, flanked by two others in full uniform.

"You're too late," I said and rose to my feet. "He took the boat in the back."

Chapter 42

SHE HADN'T LEFT. The suitcase was still in the living room by the door, ready for whenever she was. But so far, she hadn't been ready. Jean wasn't sure she'd ever be. But then, what was she supposed to do with herself?

She had called in sick at the hospital. The flu, she had said. That would give her at least a week before they began asking questions. That week had passed now, and she still hadn't gone back there. She hadn't left either. Jean had simply stayed in her house, while wondering what she was going to do, not coming up with any solution.

Harry had told her he wanted her, that he was done with Camille. It was everything she ever wanted. But was it enough? Was it too late?

Jean held her coffee cup tightly between her hands while staring at the red suitcase. On the kitchen counter, her phone was vibrating, lighting up. She reached over and grabbed it, then looked at the display. It was her sister again.

Anna had called non-stop every day since Jean was supposed to go up there and never made it. Jean had sent her a text, telling her she was having second thoughts, that she needed time, but apparently, Anna wanted to hear it from her in person or at least talk to her. Jean didn't want to talk to her since she knew just how persuasive her sister could be, and how she'd end up convincing her to go anyway. And she wasn't ready. Jean needed time to think. Think about her life, her future.

What did she want?

Jean felt her eyes fill again. She had been crying so much this past week; it was amazing there was any tears left. The phone went dead again at least for a few seconds before it lit up once more. Her sister always tried twice. In case Jean had been too far from the phone on the first try and not made it in time. Anna liked giving people second chances.

Darkness was settling upon her small street outside now as the day was about to end—yet another day where she had done absolutely nothing and made no decision. She had received an email the day before from a nursing home in Savannah. They wanted to see her for an interview next week. There was a number she was supposed to call and say if she'd be able to make it. Jean hadn't called that number yet.

Now, it was too late. At least for today. She'd call tomorrow. Probably.

Jean took her phone in her hand, then found Harry's number and stared at it. She called it, thinking she needed to talk to him; she had to know what his plans were. But he didn't pick up, as usual, and she heard his voicemail begin, then hung up.

Jean walked to the sink and put her coffee cup in it, then looked at Harry's house next door. They hadn't been there all week, and the technicians had been working over there every day, their many cars blocking the street. Except for today. Today, Harry's house had been completely quiet. Jean wondered if they were finally finished. She had no idea this type of work took this long. On TV, they always made it look like it took a few hours, and then they had the case all figured out. But it was the same with series taking place in ERs. It always seemed so simple, yet being a nurse required so much more from you. Sometimes, you were holding the hand of someone about to die; other times, you were assisting in childbirth. It was all aspects of life. And she loved that. She loved not knowing what the day would bring when she got there. It was going to be very different, working at a nursing home, where the patients were all the same till they passed away.

It'll be steady. Steady is good for you right now.

That's what her sister would say, at least.

Jean sighed. She had hoped that Harry would move back soon, but she couldn't blame him if he never wanted to. The house was a mess after what happened. The porch and the wood on the outside were completely destroyed; several windows were shattered too. It looked like something out of a war movie.

He's never coming back, is he? Nothing will ever be like it was.

No, he needs to move on too, just like you.

Jean looked at the suitcase again, then decided it was time to go. She didn't have to wait until the next morning. She could drive all night and make it there early. Determined finally to do it, she grabbed her phone, and was about to call her sister back, then put the phone in her pocket, when suddenly she heard a noise coming from the back. She walked closer to the door as the screen door slammed shut.

"Hello?"

The feeling of the cold gun against her temple made her shiver. She turned to look at the man holding the gun, then gasped. She knew those eyes staring down at her from the many barbecues at Harry's house, even though he looked different, stirred up, frightened even.

"F-Fowler?"

"That's right, my dear. I need you to come with me."

"W-why?" Jean asked. She spoke while fiddling with the phone in her pocket, frantically tapping the display, hoping to call someone, any number. As Fowler pulled her arm, forcefully, her hand slipped out of the pocket again.

"Because you matter to him. He cares about you."

Chapter 43

I FELT DEVASTATED. I had failed. I should have known Fowler would try to run. I thought he was smarter than that, knowing that most criminals that ran ended up in the morgue. But apparently not. Apparently, he thought he could be the one to break the statistics.

The fool.

I had no idea where he was, where he had run to. We had searched the canals behind his house that led to the river for hours and hours. We had the marine patrol alerted, searching all the waterways; the FBI had put a helicopter in the air and dogs on the ground. And yet we still hadn't found him. We thought we had, on several occasions, when stopping a boat similar to his, but it wasn't him.

Now, as darkness had fallen, we were lost. He could have gotten to Key West by now if he wanted to, or the Bahamas if he made it out on the open waters. I had this feeling that he hadn't gotten that far, that he would stay close. But that was just a feeling.

I sat at the docks, staring out at the Intracoastal waters,

while the marine patrol officers packed up their gear. I had been out on their boat all day and felt like the ground was still moving beneath my feet. My face had gotten sunburned, and I was very tired. I was thinking about Josie and getting home to her at my dad's place when the phone vibrated in my pocket. I pulled it out, and immediately, my heart sank.

It was Jean.

I hadn't heard from her in more than a week, ever since that day at her house, when I realized she was going to leave. I hadn't called her since I wanted to give her space. If she wanted to start over somewhere else, then so be it. There really wasn't much I could do about it. I had refrained from thinking about her all this time, well almost, as much as I was able to. But I was pretty sure she was in Savannah, and I didn't really want to talk to her right now. I let the voice mail answer it. Once she had hung up, I could see she had called more than once. I stared at the name on the display, a deep sadness washing over me.

Had I been wrong in giving her space? Hadn't I fought enough for her? Did she want me to?

I bit my cheek, contemplating this, when the voicemail showed up on the display, letting me know she had left a message. It took me a few seconds before I finally decided I wanted to hear it, and I pressed the screen.

At first, I thought it was a mistake. That she had probably just butt-dialed me since there was no voice, no one saying anything. Except, when I listened closer, I could hear a voice, one that made my blood run cold.

It was Fowler. Fowler telling her to move, while Jean whimpered and pleaded for him to let her go.

I stopped breathing while listening to this.

As the message ended, I replayed it, this time listening even closer. There was something there, a sound that I recognized. The sound of a gate slamming shut that I knew a little too well.

It was the gate to our neighborhood dock. It was located at the end of our street, and if you paid a monthly fee, you could keep your boat there. I kept a couple of kayaks in the shed down there, which I often took Josie out in, especially when she was younger. I knew the sound of that gate slamming because it always did so with such force that I feared it would crush Josie's small fingers.

"He's still here," I said and leaped to my feet. I looked at the marine patrol officer, Officer Bryant, who was packing up.

"I know where he is," I said. "Were gonna need to go back out."

Chapter 44

IT WAS hard to see anything in the darkness. The light from the marine patrol cruiser only reached a limited space out in the deep dark waters after the sun had set completely.

I had asked them to take me to our dock behind our neighborhood. Of course, Fowler was no longer there, but it was the last place I knew he had been, about half an hour or so earlier.

You could get pretty far away in half an hour in a boat, especially when hugged by darkness.

Where are you, Fowler? What have you done to Jean?

I cursed myself as I told them to try and go down the river. Why hadn't I reacted faster? Why hadn't I been better prepared for my meeting with him? I had let my feelings run away with me, let them blind me. I was angry, furious. I had felt betrayed, and it made me not think straight.

And now, Jean's life was in danger.

Why are you such an idiot!

I was surprised that Jean hadn't left since I had thought

she'd be in Savannah by now, starting her new life. But Fowler had to have known that she was still there somehow, or maybe he had just taken the chance.

He knew my weak spot, my Achilles heel.

"It's almost impossible to find anything out here at this time," Officer Bryant said.

"Just keep looking," I said. "We can't give up now."

The guy shook his head, then sighed. "As you wish."

My heart was throbbing in my chest as I worried about Jean alone with Fowler. What was his plan with her? To keep her with him as collateral to make sure I wouldn't harm him? Or did he want to hurt her to get back at me? Just how desperate was he?

I didn't know.

I stared down at my phone when it finally rang— unknown number.

"Al, talk to me."

"I traced her phone," she said.

A wave of relief washed over me, and my shoulders came down slightly. I was so scared for Jean; it was unbearable.

"And?"

"I've got her on my screen now. They're heading north of the Intracoastal waterways."

"North?" I said. That was a surprise. I was so sure he'd try and go south, getting out into the ocean and maybe heading for the Bahamas. But, of course, he knew I'd think that, and that was why he was going in the other direction. This way, he could make it up to central Florida if he sailed all night, and disappear somewhere up there, while we searched the waters south of us and maybe even went to the Bahamas.

"Yes," she said. "He's not far from Bay Harbor Islands."

I signaled to the marine patrol officer to turn around, and he did. He made a huge turn, then sped up. I kept Al on the phone as we raced across the water, the warm moist air hitting my sunburned face, wiping away the few tears that escaped my eyes, tears of worry and fear.

If anything happened to Jean, I would never forgive myself.

Chapter 45

SHE WAS LYING at the bottom of the boat. He had tied her hands behind her back. Luckily, he hadn't been smart enough to search her, and Jean prayed that they could trace her phone somehow, that someone knew she had been taken—hopefully Harry—and that they could use her phone to trace her.

But the chances were slim. She knew this much. Harry probably thought Jean had left for Savannah a week ago, so he wouldn't even be over to check on her. He would have seen that she had called, though. He would know something was up, wouldn't he?

Oh, Harry, I need your help now.

It was dark out, and Jean had no way of seeing where they were going. Water splashed down on her, raining on her face and hair. She was getting tired of the bumping. She kept knocking her head and shoulder hard against the deck every time.

Where are we going? What's he going to do with me?

Fear rushed through her, and she groaned behind the gag. Fowler towered above her by the wheel, wind blowing in his hair as he rushed the boat across the choppy waters. Jean whimpered worriedly. They had been going at it for at least an hour. Where could he be taking her? Were they going north or south?

She didn't even know.

Jean tried to fight the strips around her wrists. They were cutting deep into her skin and hurt like crazy. She kicked her legs and screamed behind the gag, but couldn't even hear herself over the roaring engine and the sound of the boat hitting the water. It didn't matter how much she screamed; Fowler couldn't even hear her.

But as she kicked her legs, her right foot hit something. She looked down and saw a stack of life jackets. She had kicked them, and now they had fallen and revealed something that was hidden beneath them, something Fowler hadn't realized was there, almost within her reach.

Jean's eyes grew wide as she looked again. She lifted her glance and glared at Fowler to make sure he hadn't seen what she was up to. He was deep into his world, steering the boat along, and didn't even notice her.

Jean wormed down toward it, slowly, her eyes steady on him, making sure he didn't suddenly turn his head and look down at her. But he was busy and, in the distance, Jean could hear the sound of another engine. Another boat was there, closing in on them.

She'd have to signal them somehow, she thought, then wormed downward. Once close enough, she stuck her foot inside one of the life jackets, then lifted it slowly into the air. She paused when she thought Fowler was about to look down at her and figure out what she was up to, but he only looked behind him, then yelled.

"Crap!"

Jean swallowed as he made a sharp turn, and she realized someone was following them, but Fowler was trying to lose them in the darkness. She lifted the life jacket and slid it up against the side, then let it dump into the water.

With a small gasp, she looked up to see if he noticed, but he was too busy looking behind him to even think about her.

So, she stuck her foot into the second life jacket, then slipped that one overboard as well.

Chapter 46

"I THINK WE LOST HIM," Officer Bryant said. "I can't see him anywhere."

I stared into the darkness, which felt like an abyss. We had been so close. We had followed Al's directions and caught up to a boat that had no lights on. But the boat had spotted us too early and made a sharp turn. Now, it seemed to be gone. I could hear the engine in the distance but couldn't figure out which way it was going. Could he have gone into one of the canals? It would be impossible for us to find out which one if he did.

I put the binoculars close to my eyes and tried to look again, but was met with nothing but darkness until there was something else. Something was bobbing up and down on the surface of the water.

"I see something," I said. "On our port side. If you can get a little closer."

The marine officer did and then slowed down as we approached something in the water. It looked like a piece of clothing, but as I stuck the push pole in the water and pulled whatever it was out, I realized it was something different.

"It's a life jacket," I said and pulled it up on the deck. "What's it doing in the water?"

"I think I see another one," Officer Bryant yelled from behind the steering wheel. He turned the boat left. "Over there!"

We approached it, and I picked that one up as well. Then I glared into the water when I spotted something a little to our right side. "Over there. There's another one. Looks like it's a trail!"

"Like freakin' Hansel and Gretel," Bryant yelled, turned the boat, and went in the direction of the jacket, fast, this time passing it since we spotted another one ahead of us.

"It's Jean," I said to myself, smiling as he sped the boat up, and I felt the strong wind in my hair. "It has her written all over it."

We followed a couple of jackets more, praying she wouldn't run out of them, then finally spotted the boat ahead of us.

"There he is," I yelled. "Don't lose him this time!"

The officer pressed the boat to its maximum, and soon we were closing in on Fowler, fast. I pulled my gun out to be ready, hoping I wouldn't have to use it on an old friend. But ready to, if it came to that.

Officer Bryant was in close contact with the chopper, and as he told it our coordinates, I could hear it approaching in the distance. I could see its lights coming up behind us as we came close to Fowler and his boat. Officer Bryant yelled into the microphone for him to stop, but, of course, Fowler didn't. He took a sharp right turn, trying to escape us when another boat joined us from that side. It was another marine patrol that had communicated with Officer Bryant. A third one came from his port side.

Fowler was surrounded.

He made another sharp turn, and now I could suddenly see Jean in the beam of light we were shining on their boat. She had lifted herself up on her knees, and with her hands tied behind her back, she was now lifting something and turning around. I narrowed my eyes to see what it was, then realized it was a gun.

Not a gun-gun, but a flare gun.

With it clutched between her hands, she turned around, so she had her back turned to Fowler before she fired the gun straight at him.

The bright red light that followed blinded us all.

THREE WEEKS LATER

Chapter 47

"DO you need more wood up there?"

I looked down at my dad in my driveway. He was wearing overalls and held a hammer in his hand. The driveway was packed with wood we had bought at Lowe's to fix up the porch and façade, leaving no room for our cars. So far, we were doing pretty well, and it wasn't looking too shabby.

Josie was in the back with Camille, talking. My dad and I were giving them their space, moving along with the fix-up. I was planning on moving back into the house a week from now, and since I was on leave from work while the investigation of Fowler and the trafficking ring was being brought to an end, I thought there would be no better time than this to get my house back to its own beautiful self. I had realized I loved this house, and now that Fowler and the rest of his goons were gone, I believed I could feel safe in there again. It was, after all, Josie's childhood home, and I'd had many wonderful memories there. I believed there were more to be made. Many more.

"Yes, hand me that big one over there," I yelled.

My dad grabbed a plank and slid it up toward me. I placed it on the porch. My dad walked up to me, wiping his forehead with his hand. He handed me a soda from our cooler box.

"Thanks," I said. "I needed that."

It was getting really hot outside. It was April, and the temperatures most days were in the mid-eighties. Not a perfect time to do house renovations, but hey, this was Florida. Any day would be too hot, right?

I drank from the bottle and ended up gulping down almost half of it.

"Looks pretty nice," my dad said, studying our work so far.

"Still a lot more on the inside once we're done out here," I said.

My dad nodded and drank.

They had come for all of them. They had arrested them at their homes, some even at the station while their colleagues watched. The FBI had taken them all down, one after another. Fowler had talked like a schoolgirl after her first kiss as soon as he was able to after being hospitalized with third-degree burns. He had spilled everything, probably making one heck of a deal with the FBI if I knew him well. They wouldn't let me in on the details. But the fact was, the ring was taken down—each and every one who had been involved, including Andrew Taylor. And the media was naturally all over it. I had even been able to re-gather everything in Kate Taylor's murder case, and Al had found the original recordings of their confession, even though Fowler believed he had deleted them. Nothing ever disappears in the digital world, as Al said. And that had proved to be to our advantage once again. Kristin Grant had been arrested too and would be charged with aiding and abetting a murder. Joan Kendrick was being charged with murder. Andrew Taylor faced charges in both cases. So far, twenty-two more people had been arrested in the trafficking ring. Meanwhile, Nick Taylor would be tried as an adult and was facing attempted murder charges along with charges for being in possession of—and producing—child pornography.

"We'll get to the inside soon enough. Maybe do a complete make-over of the living room?" my dad said, looking in through the window that he had replaced a couple of days ago. My dad was an excellent handyman and had even built the church he had been the pastor at back in the day. It had lost its roof after the last hurricane, but other than that, it was still standing after all these years. I was lucky to have him in my life.

A car with black tinted windows drove up the street, and my heart dropped. It stopped, and Agent Jackson stepped out. He smiled and approached us. I walked down the stairs, wiped my dirty hands on my jeans, then shook his.

"Looking good," he said and nodded toward the house.

"It's getting there," I said. "Can I offer you anything? A soda?"

He gave me a look, then shook his head. "No. I'm afraid we have to get going. Is she ready?"

"She's in the back with Josie. Let me get her," I said.

I walked around the house and found them sitting in the chairs on the back porch, deep in conversation. Josie saw me, then shook her head violently.

"No, Dad, no."

"It's time."

"Already?"

I exhaled. I wanted this to happen as little as she did. "I'm afraid so."

"Please, Dad, can't she stay a little longer?"

I shook my head. "It's time, Josie."

Her face darkened. Camille put her hand on her shoulder.

"It's okay, Josie."

A tear escaped our daughter's eyes. "No, it's not. Why does she have to leave and not come back?"

"Because I did some stuff, bad stuff, and now since I have told what I did and what a lot of other people did, those people want me dead."

"I know what a witness protection program is," Josie said. "I meant, why can't you come back here. To visit?"

I exhaled. This was the tough part. Camille had accepted to enter the witness protection program to start over, but it meant she wouldn't see Josie anymore. I didn't understand how she could ever make such a decision, but that was just me. For Camille, it was important to be able to create a new life.

Agent Jackson had given us these few hours to say our goodbyes.

"You ready?" he said as we walked out on the other side of the house. Camille glanced back at Josie, leaned over and kissed her forehead one last time, then nodded.

"I'm ready."

Josie whimpered, then leaned her head against my shoulder. I put my arm around her.

"We just got her back, and now she's going again," Josie said with a sniffle. "It isn't fair, you know?"

"I know, sweetie."

Camille walked up to me, lifted herself on her tippy toes, and kissed my cheek.

"Goodbye, my handsome husband. I would tell you to take good care of our daughter, but I already know you will. You'll both forget me soon enough and move on with your lives, as you should."

She then nodded toward the neighboring house, where Jean was standing on the porch. "I heard you call her when I was in my hospital room, the day you ran away from me. I see the way you two look at one another. I think you'll make a cute couple."

With that, she turned around on her heel, walked up to Agent Jackson, and let him take her to the car. She got in, and the door was closed while Josie clung to me, her body shaking. I put my arm around her, and we watched together as the car disappeared down the street, Camille waving from the rolled-down window.

That was it. She was out of our lives forever. From now on, she'd have a new name, a new place to live, and we wouldn't see her again.

Josie wiped her tears away, then hugged me tightly. "At least I got to say goodbye this time," she said.

"Are you going to be all right?"

She nodded. "Yes. Eventually."

"How about we grab us some ice cream?" my dad said from behind us.

Josie smiled vaguely, then nodded, wiping more tears away. I turned to face my dad when he nodded toward the fence where Jean was now standing.

"Not you. Just me and Josie," my dad said.

Josie sent me a look, telling me she knew what was going on, and that she approved. I knew she had just said goodbye to her mother, but she loved Jean. Her lips mouthed, "Go," and so I did.

Here goes nothing.

I ran a hand through my hair, then approached Jean. She looked adorable in her pink shirt and denim shorts. But I guess at this point, she could have had a bag over her head, and I'd think that.

"So, she's really gone, huh?" she asked.

I nodded, my eyes fixed on hers.

"You must be devastated. How's Josie?"

"I have a feeling she'll be all right," I said. "In time."

Jean smiled. "That's good."

"And you?"

"What about me?"

"Have you decided if you'll stay here or go to Savannah?"

That made her smile widely with a glint in her eyes. "I think I might stay for a while. See what happens."

I stared at her lips till it became awkward, and then I decided just to go for it, realizing that, at this point, I had nothing to lose. If I wanted her, I had to go for it; there was no other way.

So, I leaned over, grabbed her in my arms, and pulled her into a kiss.

THE END

Dear reader

Thank you for purchasing *No Other Way* (Harry Hunter #3). I was so happy finally to give you the end of Camille's story. Now, as usual, a lot of the things I put in my books are taken from real life. I recently made a new friend, and her husband works in Hyperbaric medicine. He told me about this amazing field of medicine that I had never heard about, and I started to research it more. I found this story of a young girl who nearly drowned and was dead for two hours. Once she woke up, the doctors realized she had a severe brain injury. She started treatment in a hyperbaric chamber, and months later, she was almost a normal kid for her age. It's truly remarkable. You can read more here and watch a video of her progress. It is also true that the treatment isn't FDA approved for treating brain injury, at least not yet. I, for one, hope it will be soon.

https://www.newsweek.com/eden-carlson-brain-damage-reversed-drowning-638628

Now the term Hurtcore, where someone humiliates another person and forces them to do stuff while filming themselves like Nick did to these girls, isn't something I came up with either. I wish it were. It's so awful; I really wish it was just my imagination. Recently a 22-year-old British man was arrested for doing this to a number of young girls; eleven of them were just children. He got twelve years in jail for what he did. It's apparently something that takes place all over the world, and it's nasty. You can read more here:

https://www.bbc.com/news/uk-england-merseyside-43962411

and here:

https://www.vice.com/en_uk/article/59kye3/the-repulsive-world-of-hurtcore-the-worst-crimes-imaginable

You might think that I went overboard with the trafficking ring reaching so deeply within the police department and involving the State Attorney and all that, but it actually isn't too far from a true story that recently emerged here in Florida. Doctors, lawyers, and deputies, were all arrested in a human trafficking sting. You can read about it here:

https://www.nbc4i.com/news/u-s-world/doctors-and-cops-among-277-arrested-in-human-trafficking-online-prostitution-sting-in-florida/

As always, I am so grateful for all your support. Please leave a review if you can.

Take care,

Willow

About the Author

Willow Rose is a multi-million-copy best-selling Author and an Amazon ALL-star Author of more than 70 novels.

Several of her books have reached the top 10 of ALL books on Amazon in the US, UK, and Canada. She has sold more than three million books all over the world.

She writes Mystery, Thriller, Paranormal, Romance, Suspense, Horror, Supernatural thrillers, and Fantasy.

Willow's books are fast-paced, nail-biting page turners with twists you won't see coming. That's why her fans call her The Queen of Scream.

Willow lives on Florida's Space Coast with her husband and two daughters. When she is not writing or reading, you will find her surfing and watch the dolphins play in the waves of the Atlantic Ocean.

To be the first to hear about **exclusive new releases and FREE ebooks from Willow Rose**, sign up below to be on the VIP List. (I promise not to share your email with anyone else, and I won't clutter your inbox.)

- GO HERE TO SIGN UP TO BE ON THE VIP LIST :
http://readerlinks.com/l/415254

TIRED OF TOO MANY EMAILS?
Text the word: "willowrose" to 31996 to sign up to
Willow's VIP text List to get a text alert with news about
New Releases, Giveaways, Bargains and Free books from
Willow.

FOLLOW WILLOW ROSE ON BOOKBUB:

https://www.bookbub.com/authors/willow-rose

CONNECT WITH WILLOW ONLINE:

AUTHOR WEBSITE:
Http://www.willow-rose.net
EMAIL:
madamewillowrose@gmail.com
AMAZON AUTHOR PAGE:
https://www.amazon.com/Willow-
Rose/e/B004X2WHBQ
FACEBOOK:
https://www.facebook.com/willowredrose/
TWITTER:
https://twitter.com/madamwillowrose
GOODREADS:
http://www.goodreads.com/author/show/
4804769.Willow_Rose

Printed in Great Britain
by Amazon

38520407R00116